www.tredition.de

AF185017

© 2021 Rolf Van der Wind

Verlag und Druck: tredition GmbH,
Halenreie 40-44, 22359 Hamburg

ISBN

Paperback: 978-3-347-33837-1

Hardcover: 978-3-347-33838-8

e-Book: 978-3-347-33839-5

You were my sun, the moon and all my stars.

## Chapter I

Holding on, letting go.

I f someone had screamed my name, I would not have heard it because it was raining as it only rains in this lonely part of the world, rain pouring down cold and wild on a black night.

I left her by the water's edge; I saw her disappear in the distance, watching into the darkness long after the ship was gone.

That moment I realized I was alone, nothing left behind, no hope, no sunshine. It is not the endings that will haunt me but the simple things that faded together, the little moments that made an unforgettable part of the relation fade without one final wave of goodbye.

I wanted to disappear. There was nothing to be saved, not even photographs, nothing more than the memory when this girl fell asleep in my arms. We did not care about the world around us. The feeling was so deep, so far now.

To appreciate the dignity of a relationship also implies admitting the end when it comes. I must bear the ending in my mind, accepting it in my dreams, where the aftertaste still lingers much longer, and all the acceptance cannot take it away.

I left the darkening street, starting to walk, not knowing which way to go, somehow my feet walked the way back to my house with no help from my brain. I did not know the details of tomorrow, but I had hoped for better tomorrows...I told myself, do not lose hope. What I seek, I will find. I repeated in my mind, "Trust your heart." trust those dreams that have helped me do all I have done. Trust your heart and keep hoping because I would do it for me because what I wanted to do is not necessary to prove it to anybody. Silence the world outside you, listen to your inner voice, and see with your heart, love is more significant than any difficulties we may have during one life. I wanted to stay with hope, even on a night like that. I only wanted to be there where my thoughts were clear because I wanted to be a man who has been with a girl in a yellow dress in my dreams, and I could wait for a thousand years if necessary.

All the time I was with her, I knew the precious times had to come to an end sometime. I just never thought the time of parting would be so soon.

It may have been a mistake to give up the love we had. Soon I could regret my decision but wanted to believe that I was not wrong. I tried to think that life is not full of darkness. Deep inside, I knew that she was able to wash away the pain that hurt my heart for a long, long time. I will miss her knowing that I would never see her again, and that night, I would fall asleep as if I would never wake up again because I did not know if I would.

The heavy rain made me feel less alone. Rain is a cloud falling apart drop after drop and pours its shattered pieces down on us.

It made me feel good to know I was not the only one that was falling apart. This feeling in our hearts was not going to be extinguished. There was a girl whose heart was suffering like mine. This pain-sharing time was helping us endure. We knew that being apart would destroy part of ourselves but staying would hurt us more. Parting was going to teach us more about each other. How much we can bear, how much we can endure, and how we could do what was necessary to overcome the difficulties we were facing. I may regret how we ended, but I will never regret spending over three years with her.

I passed a street and then the next. I always took different paths on my way home, but no matter how much I tried that night, I was not consciously walking.

I was only waiting to arrive and take a little comfort knowing that it was not the end but only the beginning. I tried to believe there is no real ending. It is just the place where you stop the story, a moment where you decide to change all around you. The splendid thing about breaking apart, knowing that love was still present, is that you can turn all around and forget. You can erase the page, and it will never have happened.

That night we did not take my car. We decided to stretch the little time we had together and walked to the harbor. Her name was Sharleen. Sharleen was the perfect name for her, the first time I saw her will always remain in my memory. I was attending a speech about new technologies offered at the University of Columbia. I thought for a moment she was a new student who did not know about the assigned seats, but she actually was helping the participants to find each one right place. Standing beside my table was this girl in a long yellow dress, a very vintage look that simultaneously embodied a chic and casual style. She had an elegant look and hardly any makeup. I sat down, ready to say something, but I looked again at her and realized I could not think of anything that would not be out of place or just plain stupid. The name Sharleen means free man, and in many ways, she was precisely that.

She often said to me with a sweet smile on her face, "Your loved girl is a free woman with an autonomous will." And yes, I often used to call her, girl. To keep reminding her that time did not change her; she would be eternally a girl in my eyes.

I was soon going to be home; the rain was slowing down, but I felt water all over, my clothes were completely wet. Undoubtedly as you get older, you learn that rules are made to be broken. We must be bold enough to live life on our terms and never, ever apologize for it. When it came to walking in the rain, nobody would stop me from enjoying it. My thoughts were rushing that night; they were going back and forth in time. For a second, I wondered about the future, then they went back to that day in New York. I remember we met less than a week after, and at that time, I have done nothing but investigate to inquire about her, where she lived, what she did, and where she liked to go. I guess there was a time when my interest in her could have landed me in an asylum or prison, but if this life gives me a chance...all I wanted is to take it. If we do not accept our opportunities, another may never come, and if it turns out to be a mistake? So what! This is life! A whole collection of achievements and mistakes!

From afar, through the rain, I could see the house, now returning that night was so different. I knew she would not be working in her studio; she would not smile the way she did every time I walked into the room. Be it as it may, if we are not ready to accept the challenges and the recurrent changes in our life, we would never learn to become the person we wanted to be.

How to best find ways to describe her and her influence in my life. Like in so many other things, she was a profound artist creating a world of beauty in the little things that only a real artist can perceive. For her, all she made was like poetry that is seen rather than heard or read.

Sharleen was right. She never looked nice while painting. This girl looked like unfinished art that was not supposed to look nice but make you feel something, and what she did was done with love, was well done. It took me time to see things like her. She had a way to make beauty out of the stuff that makes us weep.

In the line of work I do, numbers and code control all my assignment, and it is little room for bringing feelings into zeros and ones. Sharleen would start with something trivial, but she became original nine times out of ten without noticing it. Art is not only how you see your subject but what the artist makes others see. When I asked to explain what she was painting, she would look at me and start laughing. I might as well had asked her to explain the reason for living or asked a software system to define love. It defeats the purpose. The meaning is only apparent, thorough watching with open eyes the finished product. Work sometimes sad that captured moments into the future, moments that would have been lost into the past, glimpsed through the eyes of a soul capable of imprinting the moment on an empty canvas.

Sometimes I have the impression that she saw me as a crazy person. I did not worry if people think I am mad. "Sure, you are insane," she said to me. From the first instant I saw you, there was a kind of addicting insanity that lets other people wonder if all you say is true or just a product of not living an ordinary life. My life was not common, but sometimes I had the wish to start all over again. A good beginning would be to become an individual again and not to follow all the paths. Suppose the liberty we appreciate so much means all. In that case, it means the right to tell people what they do not want to hear, to do things another way, finding your own path is the proper foundation of liberty. I would instead be forced to the inconveniences of experiencing too much freedom than the lack of it.

As I arrived at the house and entered the room, the aroma wafted into the air from canvas and paintbrush and pens used not long ago by Sharleen. Every part of my body felt the emptiness, an emptiness I was not prepared for. Only weeks ago, we were talking about plans for the coming days. Nothing out of the ordinary, but daydreaming was a way to enjoy making plans. Simple goals like going to a nearby lake with a bicycle or walk into the next forest. Something crazier like talking to the trees, reading the memories of the many flawless leaves, taking photographs of animals, visiting a new town, and being one more insignificant pedestrian on the streets of crowded cafés, watching, talking, and searching for the next exciting shop or corner. When you do simple things and enjoy the present things, you see, you forget the world's intricacies.

Incredibly, we dealt with our lives in our unique way only a few days ago. Suddenly, exactly when the second year of the atelier's renting contract was nearing, all shattered into emptiness. Sharleen was facing a crucial moment, and I was not the supporting man I was once. We had stopped making long-term plans; I felt dreams vanishing. It is sad to give them up and watch them die. I knew the end was near. I expected nothing from the start, I expected nothing in the middle, and I expected nothing until the end. Like most of us, I know I am my own worst enemy. If I could
learn to stop waiting for things to end, most probably, I would find the happiness that has always eluded me.

A moment in the screenplay that I could have anticipated but that I was not ready for yet, a phone call that alters your whole life forever changes the road ahead. It does not often occur that someone comes along who is a true friend, but July was that special friend for Sharleen. Mostly we cannot tell the precise moment when a friendship is formed. In Sharleen's case was long ago; July was almost family. She was full of kindness, full of life. She was always there when needed. We knew July meant good in all she did.

My girl had someone who was always motivating her, motivating her to do more, travel more, and treat her the best way she knew. She was a long-time friend. She said what she honestly meant and meant what she said.

Having July come over to visit us was exciting and full of surprises, good surprises, the ones that always try to build something together, not destroy each other. If the outcome was not what we expected, at least you can say we tried, and those memories will bring us stronger together. She sometimes put pressure on us, but honestly, the kind of pressure we required. If pressure forms, diamonds also produced a diamond kind of friendship.

You might like to wait for something new to happen, something to break your routine, and when every day is as the day before, like suspended in time and going your way, something comes along that shatters your life. At that moment, you wish with every cell in your body that your day had not become so unordinary.

The night before, Sharleen told July about the hard time she was having. That she was genuinely considering stopping with the business she so much loved and, most importantly, to break a relation that was heading nowhere. Sometimes life events break your heart. It is strange how a day comes and starts like any other day, but hours later, that reality is like out of your world. This news was extremely unwelcome. There was no need to stay on the phone, and there was not really any point in trying to explain.

After hanging the phone, Sharleen stood for a couple of seconds motionless. Finally, she looked at me. Her eyes were hard, Sharleen looked as if she were about to burst into tears, but she was tough at catching herself; she would let no tears fall, Tom, she said to me, her voice very soft. "I need to go! This time I will go for the last time."

During our love affair, we parted many times, especially at the beginning. She knew about the crazy in me and found forgiveness again and again in her heart. The other factor that made her change her mind so often was that she believed that you should only break up when you are not in love. I see love differently. I think that it is also true that you can break up with someone you still love. I see an end in all we do and will do. Breaking apart is interesting. Parting breaks our hearts and frees them at the same time.

It is excruciatingly liberating to be alone. I became aware of the intensity of suffering which Sharleen could not occasionally abstain from letting me see a glimpse . . . she wanted so much more. She wanted a family, a future with no expiring date. I knew I could not let my loved girl have only half the happiness deserved. She was looking for something I could never give her. Finally, I decided that there was only one remedy, the brutal one of a complete parting.

My sudden decision not to see her anymore was utterly incomprehensible to Sharleen. She had, during the last months, one of the best times ever in a relation. What I was doing was a death sentence from a hidden and secret part of me. Fears that lingered for some time were happening now. She was being punished for loving. Nothing had changed, and then there was suddenly this. She knew we shall never be again as we were.

Waiting hurts. Postponing hurts. Not knowing which decision to take can sometimes be the gravest mistake, and in a situation like this, it was not necessary to think twice about what needed to be done. So, Sharleen said: "Tell me. What do you think? Can I get a flight tomorrow?" Frequently, the most important decisions are the most difficult to make, but I gave her a soft smile and told her, "Let us find the first boat living Cres and the fastest connection for you, I will finish what is essential, and you can start something new." I have realized that I expected to stay in control of my feelings and be something I wished maybe in my mind, but a word, a look, and all my defenses came crashing down, leaving me naked only with my natural essence. There was that moment when I realized something cannot be unbroken. I had come to accept the feeling of not knowing where I was going. And part of me learned to love it. Because it is only when you are free from the past that life offers you all. Some events leave scars with the strange power to remind us that our history is natural, but looking back, you do not find what you left behind; past hours are gone, vanquished, and the future lives.

When we said goodbye, we did not speak. I wanted to tell Sharleen: My darling, sometimes love is not enough. It does not matter which way our path takes, you will always be a part of me, and I will remain a part of you.

You were the best that happened, but lately, we were facing different directions, and love consists of the understanding that you want to grow together, going to the same future. I cannot walk with you.

Many things to say but not a sound came out of my mouth; not a sound came from her mouth. No words could say what we felt.

# Chapter II

The long sleep.

The following day, I woke up before the alarm clock went off, stuck in that strange state where your dream memory is still mixed with the present. I woke up having forgotten what it was that was hurting or why. All was disorientingly quiet, the window was open, and the air was fresh, filling the room with light filtered through the clouds. For a few seconds, I imagine she was there. My head felt heavy. I pulled myself up and out of my bed, then forced myself through the usual dawn rituals to get ready for a day that did not look to bring much happiness. That morning I wished I had not woken up from a beautiful dream and continued dreaming all day long. Sometimes waking up is full of positive feelings, but this was not the case. It was the contrary; it was more frightening than a nightmare. When you wake up, and your face is dry does not mean you did not cry during the night or in your dreams.

Have you ever heard a silence so deep you wonder if the world went missing? How you can already miss someone when you know that it was your decision, your own selfish choice to stop and never be reunited again, I had no idea. But I did. I wanted to keep my thoughts on something trivial, but nothing makes a house feel emptier than wanting someone to be there. You think that holding someone in your thoughts will bring him or her closer. You believe that you can, with memories, replace some emptiness. I realize I was thinking about the exact same idea, and it was not helping. I needed to concentrate on all the details I had to organize before leaving in the afternoon. Make calls and inform customers of the sudden change of plans.

Looking at the desert beach, I imagined talking to her, and although these words will never find her, I hoped that she knows I was thinking of her that morning. I thought about how our plans for the future made us laugh and feel close. I knew how much Sharleen loved this beautiful city, this house, walking along the long beach, listening to the waves breaking in a gentle thunder. As time went by, those same plans somehow made anything more than temporary between us seem impossible. Now I would fly to Italy, and nobody knows how long time will pass before we hear the sea's sound again.

When we came to this city, I would have agreed with anyone who said that it was very possible to find a more exciting place to settle down than this, but Sharleen always loved Cres. I saw the promise of something secret and lasting in every change in every improvement we did to the house. As more people visited us, I began to feel like a man who has sailed through a vast ocean, never knowing anything but change around him until one soul touched and changed his life. Once in a while, a dream becomes real, and now a house, a city, and the people living here were telling me that miracles were real, and that's how you know you loved someone when you know you can't experience anything without wishing the other person to be there to share it all. Solitude is fine, but like so many other things you enjoy, you feel the need to have someone to tell that isolation is pleasing.

Work! Here was the key to surviving. If you are genuinely interested in what you are doing or are about to do, you will entirely focus on it and escape other thoughts. That was the funny thing about trying to escape. The more you try, the less you really can. Maybe temporarily, but not completely. Yet, there are moments when work is the perfect escape.

Having my small software business is fascinating. It was a world of my own. I was who I was and who I wanted to be. I believe one has to escape oneself to find your true self. I might aspire to change, and I might have dared to dream about understanding myself.

I needed to call Carol. Like many commodities, talent is subject to the same demand in business, and Carol has plenty of that. For me, motivating people that work with me to let them work at their full potential is the central premise of a growing business. Carol's case was exceptional. She never claimed to be more unselfish, more generous, more dedicated, or better than other people. But she has strong beliefs, fundamental moral principles, considering the interests of the company her owns and the team's health and welfare with whom she works to be of vital importance. In a few words, she represents the sure foundation of success.

Well, it seems to me that the best working relationships, the ones that bear the most favorable results, the ones that last for many years, are frequently the ones that are rooted in friendship. I hope to look back at the people I worked with and see something more than a working relationship. Somewhere during the time, the person who was a coworker is... suddenly a friend.

I consider myself not to be blinded by success. Anyone whose goal is to succeed at what doers do faces vertigo one day. Fear of falling? No, it is acknowledging the life changes, something other than fear of losing. It is the danger of becoming something we never wanted to be. We have to recognize when success is asking for part of our soul, we must know how to defend ourselves. I train myself to deal with respect surrounding people, treat them properly. Good leaders are not selfish thinkers. Sounds so elementary and transparent, and yet it often does not happen.

My most significant anxiety was that I had been waiting for the chance to close a big deal with a company securing work that will keep us in business for a long time over the past few weeks. I had learned that waiting is the most challenging part of all, and I cannot get used to the feeling. The agony of waiting comes from knowing all the things that can go wrong. Your life is more and more an eternal waiting. It is not about enjoying life and about living and more about waiting, always waiting for something to happen.

Waiting for a call is mind-crushingly painful. You try to prepare yourself for some news and be ready, but you will never be set for the actual life because real life never happens when you are ready or never happens the way you were thinking. I felt like getting older while waiting for him to phone me. I would feel seconds bursting inside my head; time passed, turning everything to ice. The past floated before my eyes, like the stars and the moon, visible but never reachable. I was numb, too nervous, too close, and not prepared enough for what news could do. Suddenly I realized that if I stood there sitting around only waiting for this person to say something, to tell me, to be the bearer of bad news is a terrible thing. Alternatively, of worrying about what you cannot control, I should shift my energy to devising. Take responsibility for your own happiness; never put it in other people's hands. If one door closes, then some other must be opening. Do not let the presumption and opinions of other people affect your judgments. It is your life; keep doing the best you can, do what matters most to you, and make you feel alive and happy.

I knew I was not incredibly happy that morning. I knew I was using work to escape the changes that were occurring in my life. Life is, from time to time, unavoidably painful. I found comfort knowing that Sharleen was with me, even when she was not by my side. For almost four years, she held an exceptional value in my heart. I keep a special place just for her, even though I am sure I would never see her again. I long at times to reach out and hold her hand and her soft skin close to me, right over my heart like I did, exactly where it aches the most. If I could turn back the time, I do not know if I would do differently because if I had handled it differently, it does not mean I would not have other scars in my heart now. How to know if doing that would heal me or make my heartbreak in a million pieces.

Later in the afternoon, Carol called me. When uttered with just the right tone, the tone is the message. Voices have a language of their own and communicate much more than the words say. She told me, "I knew it," the company's CEO was willing to set an appointment to discuss further steps.

Miracle exits in every moment. I had always vaguely felt some of our experiences to be miracles in the sense that they are lovely. When you escape a severe accident, you do not think about the pain it may have caused, but you reflect on the miracle that helped you get better. After today, I began to believe that each moment knows its own mysteries. We can call them gifts, and that in the stricter sense, they were a manifestation of will.

The truth is that we could say this life is a wonder. Every moment you are alive is a miracle. Think of the sunrise, the sunset, the rain and snow, the moon, the stars, everything, and everyone, around you is a miracle. But we miss these everyday miracles because of overlooking or misunderstanding what is actually there, in our hands. We live in the real world and make our choices based on what is in front of us, the miracle is elsewhere, but often it is right next to us. Sometimes it is us, you, me.

My first thought was to fly the same afternoon to Bologna. It was not that everything was going my way, but I began to believe that the way it was going was perfect. If you stop to think we often become or do what we believe to be, I tried very hard to always keep an open mind. Not to limit me by my own fears and be the master of my own reality. With Sharleen, even if now was over, being open to new ideas that were one of our most vital characteristics, we continuously took the time to understand another. We knew that love is messy, just like most things in life. People or events happen that none of us could have foreseen or even understand, but we were aware of the danger. What I needed is to recognize the possibilities and challenges offered by the moment, not lose this sense of freedom because, in the end, it is all we have.

You know you are prepared for what you can do next when the possibility of misfortune is in front of you, and it doesn't matter whether it touches you. I see things as others don't see them. When businesses take an essential part in your life, something else gets lost. For a long time, I was trying to close a good business opportunity with a company in Italy, and now that my schedule was available, it seems just to be the right moment to get it done. The hopes and possibilities of today were once the doubts and impossibilities of yesterday.

So, I called Carol and told her to prepare for my trip and book a stay. She understood and talked about wanting to celebrate once I returned. "Do not let anything stand in the way of something good that shines calling your name."

Then she added, to succeed, you have to give a piece of your life that you will never, ever reclaim. She was telling me, your choice is who you choose to be, and if you are doing that, you are doing what is right. I will bring the documents to your house; you will have them all ready for your departure the following day. Do not make me wait.

"Sorry it took so long," I said. I had to search a lot to pack all and not forget something. If I were packing for a deserted island, it would be more fun. "I am sure it would," she said. I hope you collected all well and added, "I know how easily such a thing can become a mania."
Naturally, an intelligent young woman like Carol would wish to skip over the chitchat and get straight into the setting for the days I would be away. She gave me a smile and said, "Don't worry, we have all under control." You will be catching the airplane in the morning, won't you? Could you deposit this money tomorrow? I was not able to do it today. Of course, no problem, not at all, I said. Carol smiled again and said, "You've been a fantastic friend to me, Tom, and I have sort of got pleasantly used to see you. It is fun having you around. Please return soon." I said, "I will; I do not have any other plans" We walked to the door and said goodbye. I repeated goodbye, but the words are a curse because I could not utter something more meaningful to say, just a simple goodbye. Carol stopped, turning back up to look at me, and said, "Be careful."

It seemed a convenience to be traveling alone. There is always a mixture of sensations about packing. I guess you wonder if where you are going is as good as where you are. Sometimes I wonder if it's a biological need, perhaps a mental flaw, that compels me to travel. My travels do not inevitably begin with much planning. If I can include a few hours of tennis in my schedule that makes life worth living, then thinking that tomorrow I can do it all over again is a happy living! Hours on the court, always the best there is, the best there was, and the best there ever will be. Sharleen would always ask me with a touch of wonder. Could you imagine life without your sport? It actually makes sense. For her was painting her passion and not running and hitting balls. Although she was also a good tennis player.

As I early in the morning walked down the streets that remained the witness of our love, I was calling out her name. People shook their heads at the way I smile. They do not believe my insanity for Sharleen; they do not suspect the love I felt; she still made a difference in my life.

There close to the sea, we spent so many nights together. Often we took a bottle and a corner table. At the end of dreamy nights, the stars shone, the fuss stopped, everyone was engaged in their own world. But there on our table was this engaging conversation, low whisper, hopes, and secrets, something we built pretty unknowingly. Sharleen looked at me with starry eyes and whispered, "Can we keep this forever?" I wanted to have the perfect words to tell her how much she was in my life, But words could not express all I wanted to say. How could love be put into words? I knew that it was okay. She understood she saw through me and knew that our days were counted.

Okay, so, flying, I love playing tennis, but flying is relaxation to a new limit. I start, taking a deep breath and focusing on the fun. Flights are relaxed moments when the mobile phone does not ring and the Internet does not work. Hours pass in a moment, and the very lack of sensation is fascinating. It liberates me from my anxieties and guilt feelings. Since very young, I got used to seeing my father spending every free hour flying. It was the way I learned to disconnect from the world as he did from his business problems. A happy, dreamer existence, I would say, almost a foolish one, the kind that does not try to make the most of time but is satisfied with merely finding the most enjoyable way to spend the passing of time. I loved taking off, feeling the power of the engine taking us up in the sky, up and away. It is the most fun in the world. Flying is great. A kind of concentration exists that is not forced. I love to dream about flying. If we only could have wings! I would spend my time watching the earth from above.

Other people are afraid of this same experience; they say, "No. No way." I am not getting in a crazy tin can that probably could fall out of the sky at any moment. Let me stay with my feet on the ground!

Sometimes to change a situation you are in requires you to take a giant leap. But, you would not enjoy appreciating a new experience unless you are willing to transform, accept, and fall in love with it.

I was happy to be back in Italy. The land is recognized as the land of "Dolce Vita" of food and traditions. There is something magnetic about the expression that has always fascinated me.

I was going to walk inside the hotel lobby when suddenly I saw Peter Stuck. After many years of knowing him, we never had a business together, and I wanted to change that. After a short dialogue, we decided to finish the conversation at the restaurant table. Peter established his enterprise business dealing in the hay, grain, meats, and other goods. Sensing the commercial potential, he expanded to become one of the most successful entrepreneurs of the last years. Is fortune estimated by business magazines is $1.1 trillion.

During lunch, I had the time to propose a few ideas interesting to him and some of his advisors. All that I was saying was not only for him. If my words were for him, they would have been different, softer, and more meaningful. They would have been direct to him instead of to a group. He knew to understand my intentions, so I was invited to accompany him to spend a day at his house on Mikonos's island. I did not have the time to cancel the hotel reservation to inform appropriately that I would not use it.

Nevertheless, I was excited about the offer, and the rest seem to be secondary. There is a difference between the irresistible impulse and the impulse not resisted. I decided to call Carol after arriving in Greece. She and the others would like to know more details, and it was too early to tell. In the carelessness of my incessant hurry, I rushed from one thing to another, multitasking, hoping to cover all the bases, abstaining from anything that might disrupt my plans. After this, I realized that I needed to take some time off and enjoy more of what my life had to offer. I knew if I did not, what I was hurrying was my own demise. For now, I had to make sure not to lose this opportunity. We had to leave right away. Peter had his private plane waiting to take us out. Suddenly unintentionally, part of my life would be taken away from me now and would never be given back.

Even though our minds wander with love in our hearts, neither our dreams nor plans would keep destiny far away,
Suddenly a terribly loud noise and then blackness... I did not know what happened, I did not hear more...
Were there flashes of the heavens, or did I see a new star? Bright light danced on the abyss of the evening sky, was there a sparkle of heaven shining on high, whispering the echoes of a cold ocean below?

Everybody has a beating heart inside...everybody has life inside. I had no consciousness about time...thoughts flash by...about life...people, and most of all, I had confusion.

Was my last wish to stay alive in your memories and dreams when you sleep or greet you at sunset; I remember your eyes and smile. I went to your home.. every last lonely mile, but nothing was there, no you, nobody.

Asserted the time was neither wrong nor right. I have been acquainted with the light that blinds and with the darkest night. Darkness is so much more than a simple absence of light. Black is when everything you know and love is taken from you, and not even your memories are there to tell you who you are, who you were, and no one could have saved you.

# Chapter III

## Waking up.

D o not be afraid of the brokenness of the world. All things break, but not all can be mended. I woke up after three weeks of being in a coma. Everyone gets trapped by evil times that fall abruptly upon us. In my case, the airplane crashed, And only one miracle kept me alive On a commercial aircraft, the masks will drop down automatically if the cabin is being depressurized. Nothing happened that would have given you time to be prepared in the beautiful jet I was flying.

After the accident, my body has healed, memory has not. I woke up not knowing what my name was. I mean, the doctors say that I die twice. When the airplane I was on punched into the ocean, and I stopped breathing independently, and the second time a few weeks later, when someone asked my name, and I did not know the answer.

My mind was starving into obliqueness. I felt less and less. Words came, and I spoke them in my head, I was trying to find meaning, memories, but every word pulls me more into nothingness. Wishing to grab the life with a void, hoping to erase the feeling of weariness, forgetting myself completely, they were no angels or Gods, neither old nor new. Only oblivion kept me company as the coaxing whisper of fatigue was pulling me into torment.

The fact is that we are all lonely, that we all forgot who we are. Yet, another layer of my illusion is that I pretended that my loneliness was unique, that it was uniquely my own fault because I was somehow primarily hollow. My body continued to get better, and outside of the occasional irritation, I had no nightmares, no passions, no desires, and no great pains.

I was most confused. I did not really know who I was, did the fire in my soul turned into ash, my flesh turned into chaos, and my dreams and thoughts faded into blankness?

Day after day, I am less of myself and more of emptiness. The beat of life is fatiguing me.

I woke up in a private clinic where Peter Stuck's wife specially asked that I be sent. Later, I learned that I was the only survivor of the crash that cost her husband and the other three people's lives.

Charlotte Stuck came to visit me one afternoon. She was sensible and intelligent but eager in everything. She never hides her sorrows, her joys. It was easy to talk to her. Some women make us smile. She was a woman reflecting the confidence of smartness and wisdom, which, through work, strength, and dedication, together with her husband, had created a robust enterprise.

With a soft voice, she said, "I think that even if you do not know who I am someday, you will still see that I care about you." Peter told me about you coming to visit us, and I can simply say that he was keen to work with you. I am so sorry. Then after a slight pause, she added, "Sorry, it's just a word." One word that does not explain or give much counsel. Sorry means I feel your pain as my own; saying this means I take a share of it. And so it binds us together. You are mistaken, Tom, if you suppose that the actual circumstances affected me in any other way than feeling directly responsible for what happened to you. Be assured that I will do all the possible to help you. I know Peter would agree with me.

I often do not know whether a woman is a friend, an enemy, or a future lover until it is too late, but with

Charlotte, I had a sense of mutual understanding from the very beginning. How could I blame her for what happened to me? She lost half of herself that dreadful night, and here she was feeling guilty for something she had no control over.

Life was not easy for her now, nor was it happy, but she did not expect life to be easy if it was not pleasant. That was her reality now, and she accepted it as such.

There was so much agitation in my mind that I was not able to say much. My silences had not protected me, but for every accurate word spoken, for every attempt I had ever made to express those thoughts and thousands of questions unresolved in my head, confusion took the best of me. I was seeking answers which I am still desperate to find, she understood me fully. I had made contact with a woman who understood me and suffered with me. We spoke calmly; we examined the words to fit the world we all believed, bridging our differences. For both of us, it was always about timing. If it is too soon, no one understands. If it is too late, everything is forgotten.

We were two prisoners of the circumstances. Both trying to be optimistic in cases that we know to be hopeless. We did not yearn for any of this. We wished to be in a completely different truth. This was now our reality no matter we like it or not, we could not change it. There are moments in which we would wish to run away from all. We never wanted to be in it because no matter how much we
fight into this existence, we cannot comfortably fit.

She was heartily ashamed of her unpowered position.

In my eyes, she had misplaced guilt. She reflected honesty in her words. I felt for her, especially if she had the misfortune of losing so much how she could not be devastated. Some things, when they change, never do return to the way they once were.

After she left that afternoon, I felt calmer, still a traveler between life and death but calmer. I searched inside myself for silence, spending the last part of the afternoon sitting on the balcony that had a view of the park and watched the moon rise. Soon its silver reflection was cooling the earth and extinguishing the heat of the day. There was peace in the air. The idea of losing my identity was frightening and, at the same time, brought a feeling of independence from the world. Where would I find peace other than in oblivion?

One of the doctors that came to check on me that night told me: After being hit on the head, a person wanders aimlessly, unable to remember who they are or where they came from. Although this sudden and profound memory loss is rare, memory loss is a complication, a problem that affects most people to some extent.

He told me, "We will do all that is on our hands to bring you back. You are in good hands".

The time I spent with Charlotte changed something deep inside me; something I was not aware was still there. As firmly as ever, my heart was set as a spirit of man was put on a diffused future. I have no thought, no view, no hope, in life but opposed to this state is the illusion of getting my life back. I will take my peace and happiness in God's hands and cast them to the wind.

It was necessary to look forward. No matter what happened yesterday, it is not worth mentioning compared to what lies within our tomorrows. This was an offering for the sake of offering, perhaps. Anyhow, it was a gift.

I want to keep my dreams, even bad ones because I might have nothing for the rest of my nights without them. Somehow, even when you consider living the worst time in your existence, the tiniest fragments of hope survive. I got more no yesterdays than anybody. Now I need some kind of tomorrow. Survivors are not always the strongest but, more often, merely the luckiest. Adventures are only interesting once you have lived to see the end of them. Before that, they are nothing but fantasies, dreams full of excitement, and part of surviving is to move on after harsh experiences. Be happy if you are not even trying to be cheerful; what is so good about outlasting the accident? Charlotte was a ray of sunshine, an angel flying too close to the ground, like in a song, a warm summer rain, a friendly fire on a cold winter's day. I was full of energy; I would rather live than die. I would rather die than survive as a monster with no past. Where there can be a future and is a willing mind, there is hope.

Suddenly, I heard a voice in my mind telling me that staying alive is one thing, but should not live have a meaning too? Something worth living for in our lives? The voice was telling me, "Find your reason and yourself!"

The voice was right. It signifies that not only do I have to live through things, but I also have to accept all that happened and live with every second of it. The second part is much more challenging, and sometimes it takes the rest of your life to learn how to do it. But at least I am still alive.

No amount of my reasoning to explain myself was doing me any good. I did not come close to understanding what was going on inside me, so clearly, it is necessary to have faith, trust with no conditions on my planning; I would need to pull through at any cost. Talking to my inner self, I said, "I will speak some sad words to you. But you must hear them as patiently as possible. Sad words are just another beautiful expression of life. A sad story means the narrator is still alive." Life is unpredictable. Look around, today you get a rose tomorrow, you may feel the thorns. Bad things can happen and often do, but they will make the story worth reading, and anyone can survive a few sad pages. I have nothing, and I have no one. Almost immediately, I realized that it was not true, I thought I lost everything, but Charlotte showed me that there is sunshine even on the darkest nights. The accident had left me so unceremoniously empty, but I was determined to change that.

I thought about life and the sun, the moon, stars, trees, flowers, and warm days in August. I remembrance about a year ago and all the good things I must presumably have taken for granted. I thought about people I unequivocally had in my life and all the hurtful things that had replaced those simple, those essential blessings. And even though I despise the thought of crying, tears streamed down my face, miraculously crying felt good.

Comes a time when all is left for us to do is surrender to our nature's idiosyncrasies. Our identity is built upon our memories. When memory disappears, the self dissolves and the love we had with it. Dissociation is a psychological experience in which people feel disconnected from their sensory experience, sense of self, or personal history. In a deep, broad sense, it relates to a strict separation of parts of incidents. Things that used to be part of you are no more.

To live a meaningful life, humans need some answers, a particular understanding of basic existential questions. We should not be anything other than what we are, but we must be mindful of it. These answers do not have to be made entirely precise, but one can place oneself in the now and build a reasonably reliable identity. Establishing such an identity is only possible if you can tell a somewhat coherent story about the past in your life and who you intend to be the rest of the coming days.

My strategy to build my new self is not letting a day go by without asking who I am. Each time I allow a new element to enter my awareness, I should check for what kind of man it will turn me to be. I do not believe everything happens for a reason. But I still search for reasons anyway. We are looking for acceptance, companionship, and belonging, whatever you want to call it. I do not want to admit that maybe everything really is totally random, and nothing really has a profound meaning. Now I see myself as a complicated person who intends to be unique in my eyes and yet identifiable for others.

It is so easy to find justification for our errors. Do not blame others for where you are in life or your failures. Only then do you start to manifest your authentic you and what you yearn for in life. Start even if you do not have a clue how. I will stay confident and rested no matter what challenges me today, tomorrow, and every day.

I have high expectations to be able to obtain a life where someone will share happiness with me, would laugh, and the world will smile, not cold, empty, and vague like now.

In a world of emptiness, every day could be an entrance to a new life. If the new life would reflect all the expectations is open to discussion. That night my body was not ready to sleep early, and I was getting sick and tired of my emptiness. I am a quiet person who rarely opened up to strangers, but I wanted to fight my inhibition and make my feelings talk that night. I was seeking human contact, seeking the feeling of not being a ghost with nobody to touch or exchange some words.

The relaxing of my inhibitions was necessary to make it easier to bond with others. I decided to take my chances going to a small room where other patients would meet to talk before bed.

A man in his forties started telling me his story. He had a similar experience involving a short lapse of memory. His name was Patrick; he had an argument with his wife the night of the accident that left him with no memories for a day or two. Waking up, he did not remember but only fragments of the past. He told me, "It was hell and heaven mixed together." When I asked him to explain, he said, "The more facts were coming back, the more he knew how much I had screwed up his life. Not knowing was good and bad." Now his wife was asking for a divorce, and his girlfriend never came asking for him.

It did not matter with whom I spoke; life was complicated. In my case, nobody seemed to have the key to the cage in which I had imprisoned myself.

In my desperate search for an identity, I invented the characters of my partners, requiring they be what I needed of them but risking feeling devastated if they would refuse to perform the role I created in the first place. I did not want to be alone. This is the world of light and speech, and I was speaking silent to none existing people.

If I could know of just one person I loved fiercely, crazy like the wind, always like fire and rain would have been enough to calm my spirit. The void inside me was my worse enemy. I preferably wake up to the pain of losing someone I supposedly loved than stay in a cold place with a heart frozen by a lonely life.

The imaginary people in my mind were intent on escaping the abyss of nothingness I was living in. There is a fundamental difference between really loving someone and loving the idea of that person. I wanted to know of true love and, if denied to me, at least have the pain of a broken heart.

Chapter IV

Ups and downs.

I f you feel lost, sad, hesitant, or weak, return to yourself, to who you are, only in you, it is where you will find the strength to become whole again. How can I return to someone I do not know? As soon as I wake up every morning, the first thought is to find out if I can remember something. Names go through my mind, trying to see if one sounds familiar. So far, nothing! Farewells can be shattering, but returns are, without question, worse, especially arriving in a world that is not your home.

Would it ever be a time when I will be confident that somewhere in me, answers are going to emerge and that these rainy days are going to let the sunshine return? My doubts seemed justified because I was learning to accept my circumstances. Strangely, it was highly addictive and devastating at the same time. Some hard things became softer after a short while.

Perhaps depression is caused by asking oneself too many unanswerable questions. On the other hand, was it possible not to ask thousands of different questions in my actual circumstances?

Good things are definitely in my future, I'm sure of it. First, I need to find out at least my real name.

What is in a name? Shakespeare told us that which we call a rose by any other name would smell as sweet.

I think words have power on their own; a rose would continue to smell sweet, but with a different name would create another image in our brain. When did a name change what someone is? If a name is something we wear, like a shirt, I will change my name from time to time.

I asked myself what I believed. Did I pray before now? I never felt like doing some special ritual, I wish hard, but I do not pray. I can be a spiritual person to hold some beliefs, although it would be prudent to examine the different paths before dedicating myself to a specific one. Quite simply, I believe today that we have a moral responsibility to be righteous people, and that means to be fair, honest, loyal to friends, love sincerely, be someone you like to be. In short words, you should feel good being who you are. I think that should be enough.

At the end of our life, if there was indeed some god waiting there to judge me, I have confidence I will be judged on whether I had lived an authentic existence, not on whether I believed in a specific book. I cannot just conclude that because something is old, it is correct. If there was indeed a God at the end of my days, I hope he will not say, but you were never a Christian, so you are not going to enter heaven. In that case, I would be highly disappointed but would only reply. Do you know what? I am sure you must be right. I was who I was.

Religion is the one area where people consider pretending to be confident about things no human being could be sure about ever. I am well aware that we need to believe in something. Without belief, we would most probably have nothing but overwhelming chaos every day.

Again, I would never want to follow some belief blindly. We should trust our hearts, and above all, we should not lie to ourselves; immediately after saying that, I felt somewhat worried. Reality unites us, but all cultures are distinct and unique. I will not blind myself and say that we are no different. We act based on different beliefs; we judge with other laws and have different visions on the meaning of existence.

Many nonsense things will remain nonsense as long we have not yet found that point of view from which it makes sense. No matter how conscientiously we try, we cannot close our hearts forever, no matter how lost we feel. One day and probably one less expected day, someone will walk at your side, and you undisputedly have to welcome her or him! Because if you don't, there's not a point in being here.

Taking all things into consideration for the first time in my existence, I understood the meaning of the word lost. This morning, Nick Andrianakis, the person working in Stuck enterprises' security department, visited me. First, he introduced himself, explaining who he was and the reason for his visit. He told me that Mrs. Stuck personally asked him to look for my case the day after the accident.

At first, he thought that this case called for honest, old-fashioned police leg work, a work he did for more than twenty years but pausing and looking me straight into my eyes, he added, "I am astonished!" Before he could continue, I said, "You do not know a lot about me, do you?" No, you are absolutely right, I do not know anything, and I am sorry to say, it does not look good. Due to the information, we have you boarded the Bologna aircraft, but no paper was available on your person. Mr. Stuck, like many other millionaires, get special treatment and considered that the fly was within the EU borders; no complete paperwork was made or went missing. Do you remember something, anything that could help me to help you? "No, sadly, nothing I can remember," I said. He seems to have expected my answer and continued by saying, "We conceive a specific theory, and everything has to fit into that theory. If one little fact does not check, then we must throw it aside. It is always the facts that do not fit the puzzles to be of significant relevance in cases like this."

Unfortunately, the aircraft was only partially recovered, inside where no personal belongings. If we could have found your phone, we would not be in this dilemma. A smile showed hidden beneath the dark mustache that crinkled the corners of his tired eyes. Well, I don't know what else to ask at this time, be sure that I will talk to you again. I told him how much I value the efforts he and the people around him were making. "We are doing our best," Nick said. Just before leaving, he asked, "How is it, not remembering anything?" Nick laughed.

After Nick was gone, a nurse walked in, bringing the ordinary medicines. She told me that they have been informed of my departure late that afternoon and that Mrs. Stuck's secretary would pick me up.

It looks like the time for me here was coming to an end. Indeed, I was a patient for over a month, not conscious most of the time, but my body had been here without question. I would miss the nurses. Nurse, this word describes a person strong enough to dispense comfort, care, compassion, and soft enough to understand anyone, even someone like me.

The nurses, I have already learned, were the source from where I got my information. From them, I got the answers I was desperately seeking. Unlike the doctors, who keep psychological details for themselves and act like they need to be somewhere else, the nurses patiently answer me as if I was the first patient to ever walk into the hospital.

Maybe I was the worst patient. I do not understand why they feed patients pills like they were on sale at hospitals and clinics. I am not too fond when someone says, do not worry. It will not be painful, though you might experience discomfort, a term cherished by the medical profession that seems to be a synonym for anguish and pain.

Now my first memories are from the hospital. It was the unmistakable smell that hit me first. It was a sterile, purified, and very distinctive medical smell.

It took a while to grasp what was happening. I did not know what had happened; I did not have a clue. I woke up in a hospital bed. The medical personnel informed me I had an airplane accident. You were sleeping a long sleep and relax; you are OK, now we are taking care of you.

Watching the many people walk the clinic's halls, I thought about each one of them. What would all those souls here give to be out of here, assuming they even knew what that was anymore? Think that just two blocks away, people are walking, driving without a care in the world. They are jogging, doing exercise without other worries. Maybe their biggest concern is about their battery phone having only ten percent charge left.

My worries are many, if I get out of here, where will I go, what will I do. What can I do? What was I doing before?

We do not get to decide how we start in life. We do not get to designate the day we are born or to what part in this world we will go, we do not choose our families, we do not choose at all, all those things are predetermined, and we cannot accept them. In so many ways, it was the same for me now.

In my eyes, I'm kind of an alien landing on a new planet. I am coming to this lost world, searching for a dream. In the magic of a vision, I believe to be a vagabond searching for a single second of love to fill my lonely heart. Promises I will make, they will not be false, and they will not be accurate, but they will be honest. I am not coming to stay. I am not returning to who I was once. I am coming exposed to losing all of me in exchange for one instant of full awareness of the eternal truth. I may recover old memories, but I cannot return to be who I was. My short past changed the way I lived until now. I want to find a truth or more than a reality; it is the source of my own life I am seeking. I need this magic power to stay alive, and although the moment I survived, I may have made contact with it, and it has kept me here and safe. His power drains from my soul. I need it again. I require the source that offers me love, a special and unique kind of love.

The following person visiting me that afternoon was Virginia. She was the personal secretary of Mrs. Stuck. At first, she looked distant, undoubtedly elegant, the sort of girl who might have been the star of a movie as far as looks were concerned. A perfect balance of danger and charm, but there was nothing about her that was attention-seeking.

"How do I look?" I asked. She grinned. "Old and tired."
We look at each other with shy alleviation. Virginia went straight to explain who she was and her job. After the essentials were out of the table, she continued telling me that she would take me to Mrs. Stuck's vacation house and explained that I had no saying about that and beg me to take the offer. Of course, it was alleviating to know I would not be on the streets, but it came as a surprise.
Meeting Virginia, I finally knew the difference between pleasing and loving. She was not trying to better herself in my eyes; she was authentic in her ways. There was nothing fake in her.
Rejection is uncomfortable and, to avoid it, many are known to alter themselves to fit the standards of others.

Once I proved to her that I understood all she said, an expression of easiness covered her face. With a smile, she said, "I know how hard this must be for you, I wish you the best of luck, and I look forward to seeing you again." I intended to keep the conversation going, but she saw through me and, again with a sweet smile, said, "Tom, try to be ready to wait for the car at 6:00 PM, OK?" Her reading me so easy was a little embarrassing, but meeting her was a beautiful encounter anyway.

We should not dilute the potential of tomorrow. We often convince ourselves that we cannot change that our lives circumstances are out of control. That is not true; at least I want to believe that we always have a chance. Is it not peculiar, almost bizarre, that we can suddenly find moments of undeniable joy in the most troubling episodes? We have been entrusted with unmeasurable power to make positive changes in our life.

How can I find amidst a sea of souls the unique one I am looking for to walk along toward the sunset of existence? Time has taught me to trust in my dreams to see not with my eyes but my heart. I do not want others to conclude they can tell me what I can or cannot do. Limitations of others only limit my vision, obscuring my path, hiding what is there to see. If I can get rid of my self-doubt and believe, I should not worry about the road ahead, I am the road, and the road is part of me.

My body was feeling good. My memories were persistently avoiding me, but I was growing fun of not having a past. I would not classify myself as lacking in confidence, but I was ultimately out of touch with this world. I was not ready to be out there. I knew about the cost of life from TV shows, not that I could not read; I did not have an acceptable amount of time to absorb all the available data. Consequently, I decided I would accept the invitation to stay at Mrs. Stuck's house but under the condition of a predefined date of departure.

At 6:00 PM, I was ready, waiting for someone to pick me up. I felt a little nervous, leaving the people that kept me alive and safe. I was also eager to start a journey that promised only uncertainties.

I think it's much more interesting to get out in the world not knowing than to have answers which might be wrong. I had confidence in having approximate ideas and possible beliefs and different degrees of uncertainty about various things. Still, I was not sure of anything; there are too many things I did not know anything about then.

I was in love with openness, curiosity, and a willingness to embrace learning and investigating every aspect of what came my way. I did not feel afraid, not knowing things, by being lost in a mysterious universe. There were always be more questions as answers as you go on living.

Around me, others are returning to their everyday life. Most are not alone; almost everyone has someone to return to, and that is only right. My baggage is one bag and nearly empty. I wish never to have to carry more than this. I had my life, and I was living it. It was distorted, weary, uncertain, and full of mystery but also full of hopes.

Although the ocean almost ended my life, I was glad to be going to Mrs. Stuck's house by the beach. Only hours ago, Virginia had told me how beautiful the place was. I felt an exquisite pleasure listening to Virginia's opinion, but the views of others can only go so far as to where their shoreline is. I had to judge with my principles the value of everything.

It is very moving when two people come together to work something out. My life was a rollercoaster offering miracles and terrifying me almost day after day. Virginia had been another ray of light shinning to take away so much darkness from my soul. It is fascinating to me is to see people with different roots and views come together and honestly caring for others.

It is a funny thing about life when you start witnessing the things you are grateful for; you begin to lose sight of the things you lack. I missed my past, but every second I was building a new history, it felt good in some an extraordinary way.

Chapter V

Sunrises and sunsets.

T hose days I did not know what to expect.
Perhaps I did not want to find the way back to
the past. Day after day, I was finding uncertainty
fascinating.
Nothing is constant and permanent. Our lives are not on
solid foundations. You do not need to read many books to
know that. Perhaps, that is the secret, to look at your own
life and ask yourself, "Am I doing what I sincerely want?"

After John, Charlotte's brother, picked me up and drove
me to the house, we spend some hours talking. Listening
to others is a new joy that helps me to understand how
the world works.

Astonishingly, the house has a tennis court and to my
surprise, playing tennis is one thing I know definitely I can
do. There is a mixed filling that keeps me tormenting
myself. Who was I? I want to forget, and at the same
time, I have the urge to discover my old identity.

There is no greater whopping fear than the fear of
uncertainty because the unknown cannot be faced directly.
Among the trivial things I learned about myself are that I
played pretty well and enjoyed sports, I know how to drive
a car, use a computer, and most of the house appliances
in the house. Swimming was excellent, and I was grateful
that the fridge was big enough to keep me alive for years.
I am not passionate about alcoholic beverages, but I
needed the right atmosphere to be entirely confident of
this statement.

A few days ago, Virginia called and explained that a small party was about to be arranged for this weekend. So slowly, I am almost unrecognizable to the old and tired person I was at the clinic. I presumably understood the purpose of this social event and gladly accepted the idea.

Here was my life. I might never have been here before, but I was now. If I was a party person, I would most probably find out that weekend, and if I had some social disease would most surely show up soon. At my age, or more correctly speaking, at any age, we need some people interaction.

Charlotte and Virginia were the first arriving that Saturday. Individuals go to a lot of trouble to organize a party, and it is a big deal to open up your home. She explained that this would not be a party in the correct sense of the word but a more small intimate gathering of remarkable few people. Besides dancing and having something to taste, you could also enjoy one-on-one conversations, where people talk about current events and weird stuff. That was my idea of having an enjoyable time.

I felt pleased. To think that I did not have to torture myself sitting alone in a room with my habitual thoughts crossing my mind. Lately, to evade the void in my mind, I had turned to books. Books had been my most reliable companions. The more I read, the stronger my capacity for understanding. Once you have read a book you enjoyed, some parts of that book will always be with you.

The whole house was cleaned and prepared to receive the guests, some of whom were already starting to arrive. Anna, a sweet blonde girl, was one of the first to arrive. Everything was in a state of impossible perfection, and yet there were the hustle and bustle everywhere.

After a while, more people started arriving. In the beginning, it was a little torturous since I did not know a soul. Virginia was lovely, and sensing how I was feeling, she kindly introduced me to people around me.

Although some guests were related in one way or another to work, it was for no meaning a work party. Anna was one of the few that indeed worked at the company. We chatted several times during that night. As a graphic designer, she wished to be the youngest to get a personal portfolio of clients. Her interest was contagious. Almost nobody, but she did find work amazing enough to talk about.

It was marvelous to see the capacity one has to find almost at once, by a pure exchange of words, a shared sense of understanding, to which everybody faithfully sticks before advancing to the next level of the conversation.

The hostess's delicious friendliness was characterized by how many people were eager to spend time around her. I was more and more fond of her with the passing of each encounter.

"Isn't this funny? Tom, I heard someone say, come sit next to Rob. I stood up and sat next to Rob while Ellen brought her chair over to Laura. Mary grasped an hors d'oeuvre from a passing tray. She had eaten one before, but this food was too grand to pass up.

The buffet table was a blend of fascinating and captivating foods spiced Kobe beef, grilled langoustines, gray shrimps, prawns and crab legs, delicious egg rolls, chocolate cake, equally exquisite whiskeys, and wines. Kim and her brother stood at the entrance of a cozy, intimate living area space where many well-dressed, unquestionably young groups maintained a vivid conversation.

The stars glittered in the sky, and a soft breeze brought the fragrance of the sea. Slowly the number of people at the party grew. There were merging conversations and laughter and bodies moving around the pool's boundaries.

Later in the night, Charlotte took me to a smaller room witnessing the sea. She seemed more relaxed, I noticed. Charlotte smiled and said, "I always think the opening minutes of a party is the most laborious before everyone has had enough to drink and feel more at ease." She told me that it was the first time since the accident she enjoyed being in the house again. The pain was still fresh, memories still vivid in her mind.

She wanted to take the time so that we could talk about how to proceed. To stay in the house until late Sunday seemed like the most suitable decision. We agreed to find the right moment to continue our conversation.

When I went outside, I saw Virginia standing in front of a table where a man held a champagne glass. She waved at me and offered me also an iced-cold class. After introducing me to Lars Benson, she explained that she was long waiting to connect me with him. Besides being a great player, he owned a company with offices all over Europe. He explained to me about his businesses and asked if I were interested in knowing more. We decided to meet the following day around lunch and discuss the options while also taking the opportunity of playing a tennis game.

Conversation? A mystery, a wonder! It is more than just an exchange of facts; it is the art of never being bored with whom you speak, treating everything with interest, pleasing with trivialities, and being fascinating with all or nothing. This night was one of the best nights in a long time. It is the interaction with people that make life worth living.

An older gentleman led his wife out to dance, but only after she resisted for a moment. Two girls were dancing together, and Anna was so excited about the music being played that she danced without stopping. Was it only the effect of alcohol that made me believe for a brief moment that I was happy? If only there was a chance or even an opportunity disguised in my mind of finding happiness, I would accept it no matter what.

John and her girlfriend, Meredith, were standing in a corner with a glass of wine in their hands, smiling. Her nails were painted red, like her light dress that moved with the sea's breeze. She said as I passed by, "How enjoyable this time of the night, right?" Yes, indeed, this was a delicious evening. Then she added, "You must find this terribly..." "Terribly, why?" John intervened and said: There is really no need for you to be polite. Meredith thinks that all must be exhausting for you. Let us have one more glass of wine. Wine has a more pleasing sweeter taste here than in the house. "I see you are trying to deflect me from the question," I said instead, sounding honestly puzzled. I had a great night, and thank you too for coming. It did me well to be with beautiful people. What else is tonight to express other than thank you all honestly, have a sweet goodnight, then peacefully, I continue my way to the garden following the ocean's smell.

It was late now. Between the starting and the end of a party were hours when the reality was surreal, enchanted when nearly anything appears possible. There is a voice inside me that continuously whispers, I feel this is right for me.

I decided to walk to the shore, taking a slight pause from the crowded house. Thereby the sea was Anna; I think she was also looking for some rest from the excitement of the party.

"Are you enjoying the party?" I asked her. She laughed softly and said, "Too many irresistible boys with mischievous smiles and uncertain intentions. I had to get out for a little break." Smiling, I said, "I saw you dancing. And I guess I was not the only one staring at you." Anna enjoyed dancing; it was liberating for her. She looked straight in the eyes and said, "Yes, I like dancing. For I do not speak much at all."

Trying to change the subject away from her, she asked, "What about you, what do you do?" "Me? I want to be wherever the wind blows. I am starting a new chapter in my life." She had an expression of disbelieve on her face. "That is not possible. You must be that guy people were talking about; I am so sorry, I did not know." I said with a grin, "So does that mean you were talking about me too?"

"I never even knew about you before the party, I swear," said Anna. To make her feel less uncomfortable, I told her, "Do not worry, it is OK; I do not take it personally."

After a prolonged silence, she said, "I am a detached woman, making my way in a world that is mostly controlled by man; it is not easy, you know?".

I turned my face to look at her again and asked, "Do you want to accomplish something extraordinary, or do you just want to make money?" I waited for the answer, realizing that she was engaged in thoughts. She needed some time before answering.

"Why is it an either-or question?" finally murmured and added, "I want both." That was the answer I was expecting, and to my delight, she was giving it to me. "I knew you are a smart girl, Anna. It was the answer I was waiting to hear from you," I said.

The stars glittered in the sky, and the number of people at the party was getting smaller. We could still hear merging conversations and laughter coming from the garden.
"What are you going to do? Do not disappoint me, let us have one more drink. I enjoyed talking to you." She hesitated and gave a half-laugh., "Why not."

Inside the house, nothing had changed much. Everyone talked with Charlotte. Anne snatched an hors d'oeuvre from a passing tray and held one out to me. "Eat this," she said smiling, "I love them; they are exquisite." Anne was right; they were delicious.
I went to get two ice-cold champagne glasses across the room, I saw Victoria still merge in a friendly conversation with Lars.

At my return to Anne, she was signing me to hurry up. "I love this song, she said; let us dance." It took me by surprise. I did not even remember if I did dance or not. She saw my skepticism and added with a big smile, "Being tired just will not make a good enough excuse. Please! Make an effort!" I had no other option than to accept.

I believe that we learn by doing. I did not have time to practice dancing before Anne asking me to dance. All I thought was I must just let myself go to the moment. That moment in motion and the music revealed part of my past to me. Somewhere a girl must be dancing with a man, probably thinking about me.
I was dancing by the moonlight with a girl I did not know, having nothing but that single fleeting moment when I felt alive.

Trying to sound funny, I asked, "What is your name?" She answered above the roar of the music, "I am Violet, July, Rose, all the things you never thought to be dancing with." I laughed and told her, "Well, Violet, July, Rose, I am happy we met."

"I have no name," she hummed to the rhythm of the music. I grasped her with my left hand gently by her hip and her fingers with my other hand, moving a thumb along the delicate skin of her palm. "Then let me call you Girl for the rest of the night."

We keep on dancing until almost everybody was gone. During our dancing, Anne decided to free herself and danced into the wind, creating a new understanding of what it meant to enjoy the moment.

It is the heart afraid of breaking that never learns to accept risking somebody to walk in and out. In those rare moments, I wondered at the beauty of life, savoring the taste of having someone in my arms. I knew it would only end in a casual, loving encounter fueled by champagne and music. It did not matter if she would not remember about that night the following day. For me, the day ended with a mixture of feelings I did almost not know there were still existing in me.

Chapter VI

Taking a path.

The following day I woke up late. It was September, the sunshine was dancing on the sea, and the smell was unsalted and deep. As the days pass, I am developing an understanding and affection for the common everyday blessings for these simple things we should be immensely grateful for.

Not long ago, I woke up from dreams of nothingness. For some time, I was scared of everything, but life forces you to open your eyes. Beyond all the noise in your head, something tells you that you need to have the courage to risk, ignore the fear, and be willing to walk until you reach the end.

There were no longer entirely clear in my head the events of last night, but Anne did leave an impact on me. Whether anything she had said or felt was indeed the result of the instant or something with deeper meaning was still to be seeing. If I was decided to conquer dreams, I would let my deeds be my inspiration and not the illusion of what I would imagine doing. It is positive to have a vision of the best version of ourselves, but it is wise to recognize our limitations and shortcomings.

In this once distant land, I am now; I never thought I would be. I have been finding unexpected delight. I have been finding love and compassion I never suspected to experience with people thought never to meet.
If all of these are true, I should also be willing to hear wisdom from people I did not think to listen to before.

I am ready to take risks seeing what comes my way. Soon Lars is coming, and it is time for me to start my journey. Hopefully, whatever path I will follow would not necessarily require getting lost.

Undoubtedly, I will need new papers, but Charlotte promised me to help with the identification issues. I am admittedly grateful to have someone who is taken a massive weight off my shoulders at the start of this new life.

I looked at the sky. The day was warm but not hot. We had a burst of bright sunshine, but the cold breeze coming from the sea made it precisely the best tennis weather.

A red Mercedes E-Class Coupé and Cabriolet pulled up. It was the classic dream car. The inside of the car was white. The color combination makes it even more desirable. Lars sat back for a moment, then stepped out of the car and smile, seemed to be in a good mood.

I was thinking of the enjoyment of playing this game, wondering how it was possible for physical memory to perdure and other memories to get lost entirely. Playing good was so easy and natural.

Lars seems not to like losing, a widespread feeling among competitive and successful people. During moments, I thought of going easy on him, but what is the point in letting someone believe something untrue? It is better to show someone that there is more to reach.

Exchanging sides, Lars told me, "I always hated to lose. These days I am just more thoughtful about it. I am also conscious that defeats have a positive effect on me. They fuel new aspirations."

After a well-fought game, I told him that I do not value winning very much when I win; it does not mean much except that you feel good. You quickly and incorrectly assume it has something to do with your rare qualities as a sportsman. But winning only measures how long you have been practicing a sport, possibly including how hard you trained and how physically talented you are. Beyond that, we could also consider the age of a person not much more.

He was pleased that I did not go easy on him. He added, show me always what you are, and I will be your friend. Never disguise the truth, never even if it hurts. After a short meaningful silence, he asked, "What about losing? Mostly losing shows you who you are."

I did not have to think long before saying that there are two ways to deal with losing. One is blaming others or saying that you had a bad day or, even more conveniently, lousy luck. The other way is to examine the failure and concentrate on what you can improve. Losing can be helpful.

He nodded and said, "Yes, I agree. Let us enjoy the swimming pool and later get something to eat. Charlotte must be waiting for us."

Lars was right. Charlotte was waiting for us; she was ready to sit at the table alone but waited until she saw us coming. She always ate lunch on the terrace facing the beach if the weather was passable. Today was a little windy but nevertheless adequate for being outside. I approached the table and told Charlotte she was looking magnificent. She smiled and said: I like looking likable, but I can guarantee you that I always put comfort over fashion. Lars's forehead wrinkled. What do you mean, exactly? Charlotte She glanced down at her plate's contents and said: I sadly enjoy more having a good lunch with friends than going to the gym. We all laughed and started to eat. I had a salad with smoked salmon, after last night, it was indeed not necessary to eat much.

After finishing eating, our conversation turned more complicated. The matter was not irrelevant. Charlotte told me in a slow tone that she did successfully manage to get me new documents. She begged me not to ask for details, Lars who knew about the matter, looked at me and, with a blink of his eyes, told me to accept. I respectfully agreed. After a moment, Lars took the word and explained the job opportunity he had for me. During the last conversation that Peter had with Charlotte, Peter mentioned my ability to close deals. And although my business was more in the computer industry, I would have made a good lawyer. I laughed nervously. Could I have been a lawyer? Unfortunately, Peter never told Charlotte precisely the reason for my visit. She only knew that Peter was happy to bring me aboard. Another fact that Lars appreciated was my ability to speak different languages.

It was a lot to process. My head needed to absorb all. Words are pale letters grouped to give meaning to objects. As names have strength, words have power. Words can start fires, wars, or love stories. Words can let tears fall from the most hardened hearts.

Charlotte knew about my old life more than anyone I met after waking up. She had told me that as far as she knew, I was not married or had kids. Of course, Charlotte was not absolutely sure about those things. She only knew what Peter had told her the day we started the trip to Greece, and on some older occasions, my name popped up in conversation before that.

What was there to say, I was given a second chance to do something with my life, and without these extraordinary people, my existence could have been entirely other.

Life does bring darkness so often during our lives; I was down in this state of darkness. But I cannot ever say that I was alone. From the very first moment I returned and opened my eyes, I saw someone taking care of me. The real value of experiencing dark days only enlarges every slim ray of light coming your way.

After lunch, Charlotte left to go back to the city. Lars decided to take one short nap. And I went for my regular walk along the beach.
Raising my head, I see the sun's light. Thinking about those of us who are happy, those who are fortunate, we regret the passing of the hours the shortness of our days. On the other side, those who are low and blue hours seem to be empty and endless.

Walking along the beach, I wondered if someone was missing me. If I was a good businessman or even a lousy one, I must have someone close to me. Or was I may be an utterly antisocial being that never got in contact with anyone?

I imagine a unique person missing me. Today I cannot say that I miss someone immensely. No, I did not ignore you... not in a way that someone is forgotten. I think of you. Sometimes.
You left a heartache; no one can heal. I always thought that love left only memories no one could steal. But this girl of my dreams was not around, did not have a name. Maybe has never lived. I will not say that she never lived. I will want to believe she is just gone away, and a part of me is gone with her. What if during my absence she tried to turn to me, and I was not there? If we had something,

it was our life together, the only one we were going to have. My view of things has changed. Memories are all that I have left you, which may help you survive or cause you pain. I can not promise you anything, but if there ever comes a time when we will meet again, keep me in your heart, and you will try to stay in yours. For now, I wished to imagine that you just went away.

Last night, or to be more accurate, Anne gave me her phone number in the early hours of the day. I wanted to call her and see how much she remembered about the party. I attempted to tell her, "Dear Anne, come in and let the weight of the world's laying on your painful shoulders be shared by me. Your light and your worries are an inspiration to my empty soul." With her, the emptiness undoubtedly collapsed to rubble. The party had been fun and pleasing to my personality, but dancing and talking to her showed something I needed without exactly admitting it.

With this new life of mine, I expect the world to be always full of new things. But I knew that no matter how I would organize my life, at some point, I would have to grow around and between many of what life was offering. I was overconfident that my new job was taking me away from here. If I had called Anne, it would most probably be only to satisfy my curiosity, but there was not much good for her getting involved with someone already packed to leave.

I took a deep breath, let the air fill my lungs, and continued walking along the beach, dreaming of what it could have been if I had stayed there.

At my return, Lars was one more time submerged in the pool. This time we spend planning the following steps; there were so many things to clarify. I was supposed to fly to Ireland for a couple of weeks. My papers were Irish; I needed to get acquainted with a city and its surroundings while being instructed in my new job.

Later that afternoon, Lars left hopping to meet in Limerick in 4 days.

Limerick is a large city in the province of Munster in southern Ireland. The old town is known for the medieval St. Mary's Cathedral and St. John's Square with its Georgian townhouses. My sole concern was to get acquainted with us as much information about this city as possible during the few next days.

One more time, departing was not going to be easy. Every place was leaving marks on me. My memories were away from me, but there was a window open from my heart to a world that was good and loving so far.

I could hear a soul calling for me from a thousand miles apart. How could I know who I was missing if I have never met her? Could it be that existence before my new reality allowed my heart to notice her absence?

The absence of my memories was feeling like a presence, but I needed to detach of all to be free. To be disconnected is to acknowledge all without owning any of it.

Against my better judgment, I decided to call Anne before leaving. When emotions burst from an imminent departure, I needed to express or listen to a voice to calm me down. A trusted sound is essential to find the strength and peace of mind we all need. Anne was pleased to get my call. "Did I made a fool of me that night?" she asked. Having someone worried about your opinion is a sure sign that your view was not irrelevant.

I explained that the night had been a pleasure primarily because of her and mentioned my leaving for Ireland. We did not talk very long but promised each other to stay in touch.

The last night before leaving was all about me. It was about how the emptiness of my past troubled me. It was how I was learning to live with the vacuum inside me. There was pain where my yesterdays ought to be. That was my last night in the house by the sea. I was alone, felt alone, and although people were coming into my life, nobody stayed.

Chapter VII

Ireland.

As soon as arriving in a new city, I feel the need to get out no matter how tire I am. I love walking empty streets with no destination, absorbing the spirit of every building, hoping never to lose the love for the unknown. Enjoying the excitement of arriving, the sensation of belonging to the new town, and knowing I could stay forever, but acknowledging it will never happen.

I want to become more content with what I will do and leave others happier than before my arrival. I wished to have the opportunity to light a candle in the darkest moments of someone's life to return in part all the help I had received since my accident. I did not know who I was, and that did scare me. Every end of the day coming my way, I wanted to see the sunset bringing me that much nearer the goal of doing something to make this a better world. The awareness of reaching for the stars did not scare me; I had my feet on the ground.

Like so many things during the day are lovely when you do not expect them to be perfect. Only then can you fall in love with what they are. The most fascinating people we have known are those who have known failure, known suffering, known pain, known loss, and have found their way out of the harshest realities. After all their experiences, these persons find an appreciation, a sensitivity, and an understanding of life that fills them with kindness, tenderness, and a deep concern for others. Beautiful people do not just arise out of perfect life. They can be the result of challenging times.

I tremble, thinking how easy it is to be wrong about people. Seeing one tiny part of someone and confusing it for the whole is still troublesome for me. To know the cause of my actions and always expect a positive effect is a dangerous undertaking.

Nobody was at the airport waiting for me that morning. The last time I spoke to Lars, I particularly ask him to let me get on my own to the apartment he had reserved for me. The address was in my pocket, and it is much more fun to follow the indications on your phone than to grab a Taxi.

After arriving at a new place, I needed to know more. Where was the next bakery? Next supermarket? In this case, it was not necessary. To my astonishment, the fridge was not empty; it was full of consciously selected products. My new home was small but cozy. The living room was full of the morning sun. To my delight, it had a big sofa, a fireplace by a front window with a view to the top of the tress.

I was not attached to material objects, but in a way, I like to think that I was to thoughts. Thoughts are harmless unless we believe them. It is not our thoughts, but our fondness for our thoughts, that causes distress. Attaching to an idea is where the danger resides. It means thinking that and statement is true, without questioning in profound the truth in it. Be sure to find the truth before letting thoughts shape the way you live your life.

Is it maybe better to live not overthinking about what we do? Yes, like so many other things overthinking leads to problems that do not even exist. Maintaining equilibrium is mostly the best way to go.

A few days went by. I started to take long walks along the riverside. The sky's color, the wind against my face, the sunlight, and the city's smell filled the senses. What route should I take? There were so many things I found myself doing without a solid reason. It was like it was my nature dictating my ways. Why was I always using a different path to get home? Why did I prefer to walk instead of driving?

One afternoon I heard the voice of a young woman singing and playing guitar in a small café. She had a beautiful voice. I wanted to know more about her. When she took a break, I spoke to her. She was very agreeable and had a pretty friendly face. Her smile was also very kind. Time went by, and the conversation turned more personal; she explained that she was practicing songs for a wedding celebration that would happen next Sunday. I asked her if she would be coming tomorrow. She shyly asserted that she would. We agree to continue chatting tomorrow after finishing the singing.

What is what I liked about her? Was her voice? Was the friendliness in her smile?

I never thought one other person could enter the coffee shop and cure what was bothering me or that a girl could create that excitement inside my soul.

Enormously different from the way I saw myself, I have never been concerned with loneliness because I always had this terrible itch for solitude. I feel most satisfied being alone, but I knew that isolation is not at all times suitable. We could say that there exist two possibilities: either like to be alone, or we do not. Both are equally terrifying. I was in search of love in the search for a unique kind of love. I could hear myself speaking into the wind in the dark of the night, "I am here waiting for you. I love you. I never stopped loving you. I will stay with you. If you need to punish me for the pain I gave you, I will love you through that, as well. It is not your human form I am longing for but the sweet light of your soul. When the day comes, your love will vanish; I will still love you strong. If you do not need me tomorrow, I will love you, despite that. Come back and feel my pain. There is nothing this world can do to dissipate my love. I will be here for you until I die, and after I am dead, I will still love you. I am stronger than wind, and I am braver than loneliness. Nothing will ever exhaust me."

Did I know love? Have I been in love before? I was not sure if I could answer any of those questions. The worst part of not holding memories is not having pain. It is the loneliness of it. I knew it happened before; it was always going to be the same. It does not matter how all could turn out. In the end, I was going to be alone again. I needed love to keep me alive, but the pain would always come hand in hand with love.

The next afternoon while walking along the riverside, I saw her walking my way. We greet each other, and I asked if I could walk with her. She said yes, and we both went for a long walk. The conversation was honest and friendly; it felt good to talk again to a girl in that distinctive way. She was direct in her answers and somehow also enjoyed talking to a stranger. Eventually, we returned to the coffee shop where she was working and had something to drink. She sang a few songs using each break to continue talking. Aiming consequently at something else, every minute, we got a little closer in a feeling of understanding each other. The pleasures of life are sufficient to make it a delightful moment.

Since waking up in the hospital months ago, one thought was always around. Was someone in my life before? Why do I have to do this again? I knew the answer, but I wanted to tell myself a reason. The answer was easy. It is only the need for love.

I tried to tell the ghost of my old love that there was a hole in the world. A void existed in my heart where love used to be, which I find myself avoiding in the daytime and falling in as soon as the sun sets down. I miss her and will miss her again the moment she will go again away from me. The longing for love was part of me. I wished with my whole soul that I would find one day someone to love and be the one who dies in her arms.

Was Limerick turning to be more than a starting point in my professional life?

It sometimes takes a state of solitude to bring to mind what to focus all your energy on. I needed to concentrate on understanding my new job, even if my heart's loneliness was begging to bring love into existence.

I found out, and I do not know if, for the first time, that my mind's natural tendency was to be endlessly on a thousand subjects at once. Multitasking was no stranger in my way of dealing with work. During the last days, the instruction's goal was to get acquainted with a series of services the company provided in Europe and other parts of the world.

Not all that I was learning was foreign to me. That often scared something inside. Let, for example, talk about sales and how they work. Good closers must understand that the sales undertaking does not just presume one close. You are closing a client from the first conversation you or your team have with them. By understanding their buyers' goals, plans, and challenges, great closers can position their products in a way that is most compelling for their candidates from day one. Of course, sales require a vast knowledge of understanding of how the human mind works. And I was confident to understand people.

Suppose your occupation is on another line of business. In that case, all this topic is somehow dull, but be aware that if you manage to find even the teeniest interest in something, you will discover to your amusement that nothing is boring.

By nature, I seem to assume that. Closing is not an isolated part of the sales process, but you still have to be dynamic about it. When all your prospect's requests have been met, it is time to lay it all out on the table and ask your client if they are ready to buy.

I did not want gratitude to be the force for an excellent job. It was never meant to be an excuse. Neither would solve obstacles clients will put before me. Some of the most fascinating things I can bring to this job are planning and perseverance.

Aisling called me, asking if I would like to go for a walk to the riverside. I did not hesitate. We agree to meet at the same place we met the day before. The name Aisling means "dream" or "vision" and comes from the Gaelic word "aislinge." I loved the meaning.

Even though our minds stroll with love in our hearts, nobody could persuade us of the danger of falling for each other. As I arrived, she was waiting, leaning against the trunk of a tree, watching the river. If I only could go through the memories lost once again, I would know better what to say. We decided to walk for a while. Aisling whispered: looking forward to things is in my eyes, "Half the pleasure of doing them." I look at her and reply, "If you do not ask somebody to give what they cannot offer, you should be able to get all the pleasure you expect." I saw my answer perplexed her. She was occupied in deep thoughts. She exclaimed, "I like dreams, but some of my dreams were taken away from me with such a violent force. I am afraid of dreaming." "Could you answer me in the most honest way you can?" I can try, she said. "Are you a girl awaiting the world will never hurt you or a girl ready to risk being broken for a glimpse of happiness?" She starred at me and said, "I think the more significant the love, the more your heart can be broken one day." I softly took her hand for the first time and said, "If only we could feel love, a love so abounding that could never fade..."

She lay her sad eyes on me and said: But there is a beginning and end, you know? Can you escape fate?

It is not easy to accept fate, not easy to swallow beginnings and ends. If we could say: be in peace with that and all will be well, it would be too simple.

Let us believe that now is the beginning, and the end lies far ahead.

There is no love or feeling that does not involve the risk of the noxious possibility of hurting each other.

We continue strolling across small streets and crowded places, but this time, I held the soft hand of a girl, a girl called Aisling.

Every day brought new joy in my life, and at night, when the stars came out, and the moon rose in the sky, we strolled through the streets looking for a new secret place where to talk and dream. There was something very satisfying about making something grow between us. We had a magic perception about the thoughts and ambitions we searched to reach. The little things of life, sweet and simple, created an atmosphere of honest expectations. Our goals were to go for the stars; we were trying to reach infinity.

Hours, days passed having our conversations. In those quiet little places, at the edge of the world, is where we found admiration for each other. Aisling gave the meaning

I so desperately was searching for, and in the process of making our dreams come true, I forgot about the past.

One day Aisling said with excitement, "Let us go to Cork, my hometown. My parents are not living there anymore, but it would be fun anyhow." She started to tell me about hundreds of places where we could find the best restaurants in Ireland. Cork is known as the culinary capital of Ireland. Is a university town whose city center is on an island in the River Lee. And there's no better introduction to Cork's foodie scene than the incredible English Market.

With shining eyes, trying to convince me, she said, "I will show you my personal favorite Parishbrochure walk cause it will bring us to the English Market. One of the oldest in the world of its kind."

I was not aware of the many attractions the city had to offer, and it did not take a lot of persuasions to get me to embrace the idea.

We went to Cork on the weekend. She brought me to the dock from where hundreds of people left to go to America. Aisling proudly said, "I went to California, and they just loved my Irish accent in the States."

It must have been hard leaving that beautiful city to go to a faraway land. We enjoyed every hour walking around places that brought forgotten memories to Airline, memories she was happy to remember. Even little things like cupcakes turned to be significant. We had the best cupcakes in Cork, with various delicious flavors that it was hard to stop having one more, knowing that we would never taste anything as good again.

Cork was our first trip outside Limerick, but we had such a good time that we promised to keep repeating the experience of visiting other cities. How important is that you take the leap, jump high, and hard with purpose and heart to deserve the reward of your hopes.

# Chapter VIII

Days, weeks, months.

A isling knew that this day, this feeling, could not last forever. We learned to enjoy every moment consciously happy for the gift of the day. From my bedroom window, we watched many sunrises together during the following months. From her bedroom, we had a view of the sunsets. We knew that sunrises and sunsets both were not limitless. Her house and my apartment were only eleven blocks away. We spent some days at my place and some others at her home. Living in two different houses did not bother us. We understood that everything passes that our time together was counted; that was why it was so beautiful.

If you take something for granted soon, it will be harder to appreciate the value it has. When you start thinking of the moon as a common sight, you will not search for the moonlight at night. Tonight look at the moon and think: this may be my last moon I will sight. A feeling of sorrow will remind you that we are passing, not staying.

As the weeks went by, my job was taking me to different cities around Europe. Sometimes Aisling was accompanying me. She has a little shop with handmade crafts produced by artists around Europe. One could imagine a better combination of day jobs, but it would not be easy to find. Another lovely fact was Shannon. She was a college student that worked part-time at Aisling's shop. If we needed to go for more than a day, she would always be there to help.

I enjoy the liminal state between waking and sleeping, where I do not know where I am. Those seconds of consciousness that let you floating until you find yourself again. From nothing to reality is only a second measured in time. Lately, especially after waking up, I am experiencing headaches that come and go with no warning. At night when I wake up by seeking answers in corners of my mind that I would not say I like to visit during the day, I felt the guilt of not seeing medical help to find the reasons for my headaches. Maybe I was getting precognitive, and I was not too fond of it.

One cold night in March, Aisling turned to me and said, "The truth is that I will presumably end up loving you without having you at my side for a much longer time than the time we will spend together." Although she never said something like that before, the words sounded familiar. After all, I had been through over the last six months, I knew that the most important thing was that we were together. I loved what she said.

She was the girl who helped me to dream; she helped me to catch my dreams and bring them into daylight. Nothing seemed impossible. I wished I was less of a reflective man and more of a fool, only concerned of the moment and not aware of the cloudy horizon that will always end up touching even the most excellent flames.

Because I loved her better than suits a man to expect, the pain was always with me. I did not want to ignore the hurt because it was real. I wanted so much to include her in the secret part of my past.

It was impossible not to go back to older thoughts. I had left my past behind not because I did not try to remember but because every intent only failed. Aisling thought that the mistrust I had in the past, in not recognizing what once was, made it burdensome for me to live the present and create hopes for tomorrow. For the first time, I was with someone who saw life almost the way I did. She was convinced that there was no way to hold someone at our side if they wanted to go. You need to feel love to let go as much as to remain with the one you cherish. Now I was afraid that one day all my past would come back.

In the afternoon, if my work allowed escaping for a short time, I went walking to the club. To have everything near was a blessing. Aisling shop and the club were only minutes from here. Besides tennis, there was a sauna, an indoor pool. I did not see Lars very often, but if I did, it was on the court. After playing so often, his game did improve but not enough to beat me. He said: it was pointless to think about finding a way to take that silly smile from my face. We both laughed.

I introduced Aisling to him a couple of months ago. He was more than pleased with the news. He knew that from time to time, old thoughts were bringing me down. "I know that your days are not always sunny," Lars said. You can cry your heart out, and eventually, you will still be where you are. All your grief does not change a thing. Once you accept that what you had will not come back to you, you can find happiness again. This new flame is the only light strong to keep you safe. Be good to her.

Work was more than going good. Lars was astounded by how well I integrated into the team. The last sales were strong, but most importantly, I established trust with the people I was working with, which is better than any sales technique.

By the end of our sports afternoon, it was almost 6PM. I promised Aisling to drop by the shop to check the new products she was imported from Holland. When I arrived, Shannon was there too and helped unpack the newly arrived delivery. Unpacking new products was not the most exciting thing we did together, but maybe we tried to spend so many splendid hours with each other as possible, and doing so felt prudent.

It is breathtaking to acknowledge the power of creation originated from artists around the world. I am not stunned by the power of bringing into existence by the artists who are the obvious ones working with paint, clay, wood, and so many other materials, including words. I am stupefied by the creativity of the soul.

The hours went by between examining new pieces of merchandise and unshapely conversation with the speed that goes by only when you are having an agreeable time. It was only right to invite Shannon to come with us and relax while having something to eat at some restaurant in the neighborhood.

Sitting at a table by the window, Aisling went through a mental list of what she wanted to order. Some asparagus salad and vegetables would be enough for her. We did not eat much in the night, but later we also asked for pancakes with strawberries and raspberries. Something sweet was always welcome. Shannon was more into Italian food that evening; we both had some pasta.

I knew from Aisling that Shannon was an eager student, so I asked her how college was. Usually, when you ask this, they say, is excellent, but I was surprised by the answer. She said that in the beginning, she was very enthusiastic. The world was in front of her waiting to be discovered, but soon she found that college was not the romantic place envisioned before. Many of the dreams faded, and she found herself in an institution that demanded more to study instead of asking questions. I can understand this point of view. We require absorbing volumes of information from day to day, and there is a small room left for questioning the topics.

How Aisling and Shannon became friends was well known; now, a particular relation emerged that grew stronger each day. Cutting people out of your life is indeed artless. Keeping a friendship is not. Aisling told me once that Shannon was a soulmate. It is considered unusual to find someone who sees the same world you see similarly. Most people do not want a friendship that comes and goes at the caprice of emotions. Aisling said firmly, "You know how much we depend on her, and I know we can always count on Shannon." And with feelings of thankfulness in her voice added, "We do it for each other, not wanting something in return, except allowing us to grow closer."

It was getting late when we decided to go. Luckily Shannon did not have long to walk. She kissed Aisling and, facing us, said, "I swear from the bottom of my heart I want to see you both together for the longest time." We thanked her and went separate ways.

It was pleasant to walk that night. Now it was still cold, but you could notice the winter coming to an end. We continue talking about friendship while holding her hand inside my jacket. Aisling did not have many friends, but she was proud of that. If you say you have many friends in her eyes, it was a sure sign that you did not really know anyone in deep. She genuinely preferred to have a few friends but true ones.

I asked, "Do you feel the spring coming?" With the spring approaching, she was under the impression that there can not be problems except where to be happiest.

When are you flying to Madrid? She wanted to know. I told her that by the end of next week and added, I would like to learn if you could take a few days off. Is that not a great idea? "Yes, yes, yes," was all she said.

Upon arriving at my apartment, we seal our plans to fly to Madrid, but I insisted that she come two days after me. I did not want to let work disrupt my attention. I wanted to be indivisibly attending her.

When my eyes met her lovely face and her unblinking look reflected at me, time stopped. Long I had wished for someone to fill the vacuum inside my heart, and the effect on me was immeasurable. Now there was no past and no future. We had each other. This was our present.

With every step, every minute, we became more dependent on the walks hand in hand, the lunches in our favorite place, the smiles, the caresses; we had passion following our path, taking to the air of this and that.

It was good to be home. It is a delightful sensation to come back to something familiar. I went to take a hot shower noticing the silence around. For me having a long hot shower at night was therapy. With every drop, the day's stress and the worries of work went away drop after drop. We made the room dark. All was so peaceful; there was no sound to distract us from being close. In our bed, very close to each other, we laid down and closed our eyes. Both happy, for we have lived today.

The following day I left her sleeping with her hand across her forehead, looking relaxed and content. One of the convenient aspects of having a shop was that she was able to sleep until late. Of all the things she did, sleep probably provided her more than anything with uninterrupted inspiration. As soon as she opened her eyes, a thousand ideas came pouring into her mind. Possibly in her dreams, she toured all the places she was so eager to discover.

I was delighted not to have woken during the night. My headaches forgot to visit me. I wanted to be like other men, not haunted by the past or uncertain of the future.

I started planning a lot at the office, but I actually did nothing of all the plans. Naturally, I like to think that if I did not have a well-thought strategy, I would hardly arrive at the destination, but ultimately this means nothing if you did not take into account the unexpected. Two of the leading persons included in my plans called announcing they were sick. Spontaneity is one of the delights of continuity. For me, it meant time to do things you postponed a hundred times before. With John and Katy, two of the best coworkers, we organize a three-day workshop about "Creating genuine urgency." In our industry, this reflects the notion that salespeople who reliably attain the goal never entrust on the promise of a price cut to get the transaction done. They know the price should never be the initial reason to buy right now instead of next week, next month, or next year. Alternatively, they find a legitimate, pressing issue or opportunity related to their product.

Once they have helped their client understand it favors them to purchase instantly, they can work with them to figure out the exact terms.

The atmosphere at work was a good sign of a team doing a good job.

The night before leaving for Madrid, we wanted to go out and do something distinct, something memorable. Aisling wanted to go to the theater. Theaters are curious places, the day you want to go, they did not offer any remarkable play, but all seem exciting if you do not plan to go. We decided to go to the opera instead of the theater.

For the first time, to her displeasure, she discovered that they were singing in Italian, and since she did not know a single word, it was like we were transported to Rome. We had quite a fun time, but people did not appreciate her constant giggling. They say that all true opera lovers cry, Aisling was not much of an opera lover.

We just wanted to write in our hearts that every moment was the best moment. Joy was not in another hour or place but in every minute we were spending together. It was not the events that made us happy. Every little smile, every look into each other's eye, had the power to make us happy or unhappy tonight. It was our way to survive eternity, to press eternity into one single kiss.

Aisling and I were having the best time of our life. We were exactly the opposite of a broken heart. So many people could not understand why their hearts were breaking. Every broken heart has screamed, "I need to know why?" We wanted to shout, "We wanted to know why we could not continue like this forever?" That what we had; that was always meant to happen. There was no way to know what makes one thing occur and why not another. It was unusual how well our view of the world was reflected in our beliefs. We knew that a complete stranger could alter the life of another irrevocably. Not long ago, we collided and changed the rest of our life.

We had the world on our feet; how foolish not to believe we were more powerful than the moon, the sun, or the stars.

We liked to have the same view about fate. Knowing that we both, no matter what we did, our destiny was coming for us one day. We appreciate the freedom of choice, of taking our decisions, but we never blinded ourselves to believe in endless days of glory.

If our whole life was formed to this meeting with each other, something must be willing to explain the meaning of loving.

No matter how happy my life was with Aisling, the thought that I had no past was alive and that I could never have anticipated that this was the only way to bring me to her. Maybe we were always bound to end up exactly where we were.

But that was life with all the miracles, surprises, and pain to keep us cultivated in an eternal wonder. I thought of life taking unexpected turns, sometimes during our random decisions. If an inner decision is not made consciously, it appears outside as fate. It was sometimes a fluke and mostly a destiny, but I am sure finding myself with this girl made me smile whatever it was.

Chapter IX

Close to heaven and hell.

That year, the spring came suddenly to us in Ireland, but it was already here in Spain where I had been the last two days. The days were so clear and the skies so brilliant blue, with only a few white clouds hanging around. The air tasted fresh and delicious, everywhere the smell of grass and flowers. I did not know that the wind could be warm, the clouds so happy to let the sunshine. Then sometimes in late March, you knew springtime was here to stay.

I had never assumed so unquestionably the consequences of losing my memory. I lived a dream of existence. I was having the perfect relationship and looking with hope into the future. At that very moment, I realized that although many questions would probably never see an answer, I was happy.

Could it be possible? Maybe something inside me had to die so that a new me could be born from the ashes of my old me. So many days, I did not know where I was. I was a vagabond without a shred of a notion that all was going to change.

The day I found my smile again was when I heard her voice singing in a small coffee shop. From that moment, the rest of my days shifted to a new high.

We cannot even presume to understand the intricate powers behind every event that occurs in our lives. If you want to break out of the ordinary, you must learn to think and dream the impossible. And in this case, not only learn to think and dream but learn to love the dreamer.

Nothing ever happens like you presume it will. That is one characteristic of life, and I came to accept it until something shows you were never ready.

Work was not going well as in previous times. The company we wanted to have as a client was hesitant. We needed to create more urgency, and how to do that was not clear.

Last night as I spoke with Aisling, I told her, "It is tender, loving you from afar, but I need you here at my side." She said, "I will be there tomorrow; I deserve the spring, here it is still cold and gray."

Before saying goodnight, I said, "You are the centerpiece of who I am, what I do, I cannot live without you." There was a brief silence, and then she said, "I do not like days without you. Everything turns invisible around me because of your absence."

Before I was able to speak, she continued saying, "I do not want to be without you. I like who I am with you; an entire world of people can never replace you. Good night, love".

It was hard to concentrate on work while counting the minutes until she would return. My thoughts were always going back to something she said or did, like the night before I left when she asked me, "What would you do without me?" The question was the desire to hear how much she meant to me. We had tangled ourselves in the sheets of her bed, watching the sun going down. It was one of those nights that we made love before even saying hello returning from work. I put my lips so close to her ear and, softly biting her earlobe, said, "I love you. To live with you is to live. Life is cruel death to me without you. I do not want to go back to who I was before finding you." She wanted to know more about it and was going to ask me something, but I tenderly slid one of my hands between her knees, and my fingers began floating up and down her inner thigh making her brain get blurred and forcing her to forget about asking more questions. It was more pleasurable for her to feel my desire than hearing me explain it with words.

It was around 11 AM when I received a call informing me Aisling had a car accident. Nobody can shield you from the unexpected, but it breaks you; it knocks you off anyway. A deep but calm voice on the phone told me she was alive but unconscious.

There was not much information available at that moment. I only knew that Aisling was a passenger in the car, taking her to the airport.

To give love and get loved is the reason you are here on earth. Everything else lost importance in the blink of an eye. There was no way I would stay. It was no way I could focus on my work. I had to return.

I wanted the perfect finishing days in Madrid. Now I had ascertained the hard way that some wishes stay unfulfilled. I needed to be by her side. I cared infinitely about her safeness that I felt as though I was going to bleed out with the idea of losing her. Why did I not allowed her to fly with me? No amount of lamenting can change the past, but it is easy to regret some choices. It is one thing to want to do things your way, but it is another to think that your perfect draft is the only one right.

The only person I thought to call was Shannon. My heart pounded faster and faster. Pain spread, and joy diminished. I needed her to tell me that all was good and that Aisling would be returning to me that what we had planned was only postponed for some hours. When Shannon finally answered the phone, her voice was calm. "Tom, I am here at the hospital, and there is not much I can tell you. I am devastated, but I know she will make it; she must," she said.

The hours were fogged and slow like not even time wanted to understand what was going on. I glanced out the window at the signs of spring, something to distract my mind, but nothing could take my worries away. Nothing could affect my life so much than Aisling having hers affected by something unforeseen.

Aisling, wait for me; I am coming to be by your side. How desperately I long to be by her and hold her hand. To tell her, "Everything will be OK." The part that makes it so hard to accept when a dream is taking away from you by sheer chance is that you find yourself living in a reality that is so different from the one you expected. One second is all life needs, one second that suddenly alters everything. A pain stabbed my heart. Again something was changing my world.

I saw Shannon from a distance. She was strangely absent. When people gaze in confusion is because they do not understand the world. Other people were there, people I did not know. When she saw me, she came rushing into my arms and embraced me. I held still, waiting for her to say something; finally, she looked at me and said, "She is gone."

I have no memories of what happened after that. I did not care to see who was in that room. There was only one wish in my mind, and it was to disappear to vanish, if possible, forever. Grief is the price we pay for love.

I never returned to her house. I never saw another sunset from her bedroom. To everyone, understanding that my life was changing was easy that my broken heart needed solitude. Nobody understood.

Outside, the birds were coming back, and the flowers coming out, and the air was full of the sunrise scents, and inside me, everything was dying, the light was fading, my hearth whitening.

I could feel my body descending to the darkest and coldest hell. My hopes and dreams left me too. Knowing that things will never be the same ever again reinforced the destruction of myself.

I was trying so hard to recover my memories, and suddenly, I needed time to forget my mangled heart and push away the torturous memories. Soon I would barely remember that the world was a place different from the abyss I was breathing.

Only months ago, we had first come into the full knowledge that we loved each other and wanted to stay together for as long as our love would allow us.

Now, there was nothing I could understand, nothing to come back to, nothing to look forward to, because everything happening was real; it was our end, an end for all eternity.

The funeral was to be next Tuesday, but I never contemplated going. I wish to state with all sincerity that I do not want to go to any religious ceremonies performed after her death. I do not believe in such rituals. In the emptiness that was all around me, others opinion was the least of my concerns.

Only Shannon was able to talk with me during those days. She asked me once, "Why did I not want to go and say my last goodbye." I said, "Funerals are not for the dead. If they are of any benefit, it is only for the living." My ears could not bear people saying, "Poor girl," when those two words symbolized Aisling, a girl to whom I gave my undivided love, full of hours, minutes, beautiful moments, of hopes, smiles, and kisses I will never have again.

I don't want to end on the ground. I want to be burned and scattered over the ocean so that my grave will be nowhere. No one should ever come or put flowers and grieve.

Those days I needed to feel the pain. I needed my suffering to keep hurting me until I realize that I never needed to break in the first place. I never understood people that reject their belief after losing a beloved one. All kinds of lives get lost every day. Young and older people of every age die, but they do not question faith. Why, only when they loved one, do they complain and ask for reasons?

Pain is a healer. If you do not lose a part of yourself, then you will feel no pain. Rivers of tears will not change what happened; only will show how much of you went away. I need to be honest with my heart, suffer, and break as needed.

I decided to quit my job and leave the city. To walk alone along the streets was hurting me too much. I saw Aisling in every corner, in every place. She will always live in my heart, and in an unusual hope of life after this, I wished she would have a place in her heart for me.

Breaking up with someone you love hurts and can destroy you in many ways. Sometimes you recover from pain; sometimes, you do not. But breaking up is a choice one that can get reverted if both agree. Death is final.

The last time I saw Shannon, we sat in silence, letting the green and the sun in the air heal what it could. I wanted to tell her that I was grateful for the time with her, but I felt revolted at life, and I only was able to say that we cannot spend time; it only can be squandered.

She asked me, "Why do you not want to stay here?" I took her hand and, looking in her eyes, said, "The only place I ever felt at home was here with her. Here is not a place for me anymore; anywhere else will also not be." She had tears in her eyes; I had tears in my eyes.

Love knows not its depth until the moment you must say farewell. We spoke so many times about the briefness of existence. It was as if we knew we would not have all the time we wished for in our love story. What hurts most is that life did not give us enough time, did not give us not a warning, and did not give us the chance to say goodbye. Those are the ones causing the severest pain; the goodbyes never said.

I was feeling emptier than the day I woke up in a hospital bed. Neither the angels above could help me understand, nor the demons down under had an answer for me.

I wanted to say goodbye, but she left before I could have held her hand and kiss her lips for the last time.
Now my words would travel through ages and never reach her ears. The wind would take all, and nobody would know of the meaning.

I wished I could have told her, "My only love, this is not a goodbye; it is my way of thanking you for all of you. You came into my life when I was lost and alone, bringing joy and giving me a reason to be alive. Thank you for giving me memories. I will cherish them forever. And most of all, thank you for teaching me to be prepared for our ending.

All the hours you spend talking about the shortness of existence now, I see you were telling me it would come a time when I can ultimately let you go. I love forever, my girl."

Chapter X

Changes.

F arewells can be agonizing, but returning to you old, you are worse. It is paralyzing. Every tiny droplet of realization brought pain. It has taken me weeks to accept that her absence in my life was beyond the bounds of possibility to change. Guilt was all around me, the regret of not telling her, "I love you" one million more times, the remorse of not being able to feel happy today, knowing that this day shall never return. My reasoning was telling me to continue living because she would always be a part of me, but my heart was broken into too many pieces.

I believe in love, in the power of a smile, in things I can't put into words, in something I know to be true. During the last seven weeks, I have been drifting from one place to another, trying to find the way back in this void from where no one is allowed to return.

Liepaja is the perfect place for me to be today. The long beach with plenty of space is ideal for my present state of mind. I rented a room in a hotel close to the beach near several restaurants and the market.

Real change requires sacrifice. Some parts of me will never harmonize with my new way of living. I am decided not to fall in love again, never return to seek love. What was far away is near me today. I know what love is, what pain is, and what grief feels like. Now I need to disassociate from those emotions for a moment.

Living with indifference to all the actions and passions of society was not assumed to be such a remarkable quality,

I guess, I knew that deep inside, but it was a way to survive for now.

After I started working with Lars, I told myself, "Never let money rule your life." Now, I was looking to make money, not for the sake of accumulating wealth but to place my full attention on something tangible. What is the point in amassing money? One day the greatest regrets in life will not be your failures at work. On the contrary, hard times will make you proud. The greatest regret by far will be acknowledging the amount of time you spent in pursuing vain things.

In time, they tell me, I will heal and live again, but I do not want to overcome the pain. There is a reason I feel like this, and I accepted.

For now, I needed to occupy my thoughts, discerning how to go back to work. I placed several calls to people I met during my time in Ireland and started offering my services as a consultant. Part of me knew that before my accident, I must have worked doing something similar, every aspect of this business was so natural to me.

To the people working with me, I said nothing about the turmoil inside myself. Only my fingertips could feel the scars left in my heart. I pretended to irradiate confidence and trust to the outside, but only tears there were inside. I felt very calm and very empty. Work cannot replace or feel the space left behind by someone who was once the center of the universe.

Life can turn into a suspended state of torment. If you keep living like someone controlled by this state, you keep going on, day after day, until you collapse and die.

Happiness is not merely having our material needs met. You can find satisfaction in good food, music, art, or sexual pleasure, but one day you realize that all those things do not fulfill your heart. This world offers you other rewards where you supposedly can find meaning like social recognition, status, etc. Perhaps some people could confuse all of this with self-fulfillment, but if the acts did not originate in your heart, you would spend your all life following other people's demands and never lived a life of your own.

365 days after starting a second life, the only thing I know is that everything you love will die. The success I was having doing my work was not going to last forever. I felt the urgent need to detach myself from the things I was doing. Detachment is giving the best of you but accepting the truth of being replaceable and consistently aware that nothing is permanent. Do not let your ego make you believe. Not everything is about you.

The days and weeks passed, but I never forgot. It is hard to ignore Aisling's memories when there is such an empty space inside me.

Seeing that my headaches were coming more often, I decided not to postpone a doctor's visit. As far as I can remember, my health was excellent and stable. Of course, nobody wishes to be sick. You do not decide to be sick. I would also agree by saying the same about drug addicts. Many people tried drugs as a matter of curiosity. Only to find themselves being addicted to narcotics after a more extended period of continuous use of them. One morning you wake up, and you discover that an addict is all you are. Probably you also do not wake up being sick without any warnings. Your body sends you alerts we fail to recognize or take seriously.

For now, my work was satisfying and an escape from all. Before going to sleep, thoughts visit me reminiscing beautiful times so far gone now, but Aisling was like home. I always found a way back to her. I miss that feeling of connection. Knowing that at the end of the day, we would still be together.

Strong wind and rain on the rooftop of the house gently pull me toward consciousness. I struggle to return to sleep; nonetheless, I am vaguely aware that my headaches were more substantial.

I assumed that the "lingering headaches" I had been suffering were due to the accident, but I decided to look into the cause more diligently.

During checkup in the CT Scan, they noticed abnormalities and requested an MRI to test the anomaly. Later the same day, close to midnight, they confirmed I have a mass in my brain, most likely a tumor.

What was causing my headaches had nothing to do with the accident. It was because I had a 5 cm brain tumor that appeared to be very aggressive. Doctors said I have a mutant glioma, a rare brain cancer that is notoriously difficult to treat. They said I was not going to make it, that I only had a few weeks to live.

To get used to the horrifying revelation and the gross disparity of life around you is not untroublesome. It was unbearable for me to conceive the rest of my life without Aisling, but now I only have to live it.

I walk until there were not more houses, all the way to the part of the beach where you could not see but the sea and the sky. The night was dark, warm, and clear so that looking into the night, you could see a million stars.

I will allow myself to feel love again. Implying love in the vastest meaning. Not limited to a relation between man and woman but devotion to humanity. What else could I do? That thought frightened me, yes, love in a way

I had once sworn to myself I would never consider pursuing. I had become entirely defenseless, torn apart with hurt, and tossed onto a path I might never have taken otherwise.

I made it my calling to help people in dark periods in their life see the light to reveal life has meaning. And in the process of assisting others to recover the meaning of mine.

Time is precious, but what you do with the time you have could be more precious still. I did not wish to go gentle into the night. I did feel resentment from the approaching darkness. To hate is to be blinded but to want to fight is your right. How could I hate the life I had? All the pain was brought by the pleasure of having had the best that life has to offer. So there was no place in my heart to hate what was happening to me now.

It is best as one grows older to strip oneself of poisonous thoughts caused by broken dreams or unexpected turns in life. I felt sure that I was going mad again, having to face another demon, but by now, something in me was less afraid, less perturbed, and less affected by my fate.

Perhaps the bravest thing I have ever done was to keep my hope up after losing all my past or continuing living after Aisling's death when I wanted to die. Nothing I do would ever change the things we so fondly loved together. She is not here, but all is untouched, unchanged forever in my heart.

Death gently twitches my ear, and I can hear it say to me, "Do not simply wait for me; use the time you have to live forever."

We should not burn our names on a stone if we can burn it on people's minds. I knew my situation was not ideal, but the journey was not yet over; it was going on, it was not the end, but part of the road.

It seems like a long time ago now. I woke up alone in an unknown room with not one memory of whom I was, and here I am again alone, but this time, the memory of Aisling is with me to make the new start more comforting. Her words resonate in me; they guide and inspire me to continue.

A memory came to me from a message you once sent me after asking her if she would like to go somewhere. She wrote something like, "Yes, of course, I love Valencia. Valencia is located in the very south, and there it is similar to Sicily. The weather, the fruits, and warm climate, the culture, this Arabic that mixes with European culture, so I know the whole corner there, Malta, Sicily, the small islands in the Mediterranean Sea, Ustica, what interests me is the history of the Mediterranean Sea" She loved that region. I said to myself, "OK, let her guide you. Go and visit the Mediterranean."

Time does not heal all wounds. Aisling was starting to feel like a friend that went away, not only the source of pain. Going where she wanted to go could help to feel her closer, and who knows whether going there may not end being the greatest of all blessings.

Chapter XI


Flashbacks.


D isconcerted about how to face the hugeness of my task, I traveled from the northern part of Europe to the warmer south. Of all the seasons, autumn is the one I love most. The melancholy of the summer endings and the start of colder days always made me nostalgic. Rain makes me feel less alone, and waking in the rain is a pleasure most people avoid appreciating its beauty.

Arriving, the sun did not shine. A big long cloud was over my head that stretched out to the horizon, and at the end of it, the sun was slowly descending, sending colors of red, yellow, and white all over the city. As always, my first impulse was to walk and keep strolling until finding the right place to stay.

Waking across Pula, a coastal town on the tip of Istria's Croatian peninsula, I saw a painting hanging in the window of a shop that shook me deeply. As if some old part of myself woke up in me, petrified, useless in the life I had then. I knew this painting; I was sure about it. Frightened of what the next moment would bring but more fearful of not doing anything. All these sensations and images coming out of this artwork were so vivid, impossible to resist. I walked into the art gallery and asked the owner about the painting. The older man told me, "I am sorry, but the painting is not for sale." After explaining to him, he allowed me to take a picture and gave me a paper with an address to find more about this piece.

A shock could destroy the fabric of time. Furthermore, trauma can be a one-off, unexpected event such as a traffic accident but in my case, it was bringing back memories long forgotten. To waste the time I have in this body, running away from discovering about my past is the most deadly thing I could have done, so I decided to investigate and find out about the painter. I was never, and in no way, going to let go of the one chance I had to fix myself.

Life has a way of wilting, flowering, and surprising at the strangest, unpredictable places and, most random occasions. This painting appeared from nowhere, leaving more open questions. I would never allow my hopes to evaporate. I was ready to travel thousands of miles against hurricane winds for the opportunity to find the past.

The new destination was Rabac. This romantic resort located on the Istria region's east coast was not familiar to me, but something was bringing vague memories back. It was something in the surroundings that seemed known. I first started to remember specific memories of streets, although I was not entirely sure if my mind was clowning me. A house from the photograph came back to me. I tried to drive it away and focus on the present, but I was in the past, my heart started beating faster, and my throat was dry. In front of me was a small shop full of artwork. As soon as I enter the store, a too familiar smell invaded me, the smell of paint, brushes, oil, and canvas. During the time I spent inquiring about the painting, I revived the past, although it was happening in the present. Finally, I had a name, Sharleen Johnson.

My shoes walked towards the old part of town. I felt as though I were dreaming. Terrible anxiety increased the beat of my heart, and for the first time since the accident, the sweat upon my forehead was a sign that old memories were resurfacing. Now, forgetting was more comfortable than remembering. Who could tell what was lying ahead in the next few days?

With my newfound sense of remembering came strange thoughts and instants of visions flashing in my head. I did not understand or recognize all the bits, but my nights were restless and agitated.

During hours of turmoil Aisling helped me to calm down my frenetic heart. The first day I touched her, knowing I had no past, she started giving me memories. While strolling through the streets, she prepared me with her vision of life for her departure. Now she led me to my past. How could I ever forget the sweetest girl who loved me?

The next city on my schedule was Opatija. Opatija is a Croatian coastal city on the Adriatic Sea. After researching on the Internet, I knew about Sharleen Johnson enough to contact people close to her. The desire to walk around the city was habitual for me, and now it was necessary to walk around, hoping to find more clues.

This remolding in my doing is not an attempt to avoid thinking about the limited time I had left. My real intention was to bring all the pieces together.

As I was walking through the pedestrian zone, I heard someone calling "Tom, Tom." I turned around, and a girl I did not know embraced me. She had a sweet smile and tears in her eyes. She hugged me tidy, and then she let go starting to hit me in my chest, saying, "Why, why did you go?" People around us looked amazed at our scene. Why was she talking English to me? Why was she calling me Tom? I did not know what to say. And at that moment, the only serious thought that arose in my mind was to ask, "Are you an artist, are you, Sharleen Johnson?" She looked at me, perplexed, and said, "What are you saying?" I begged her to stay calm and listen to me. Her face was not smiling anymore; her look was awkward but delicate. She asked, "Do not you know who am I?" I said, "Sorry, but I do not remember."

We went to a coffee shop and talked for a long time. It is bizarre how your brain can play tricks on you. You might be having a somehow allowable morning, and then this wave of truth comes over you so strong you do not know who you are anymore. Of course, the girl I was talking to was Carol. She told me all about me. She even showed me pictures of Sharleen and me on her phone. Photos about people that worked with me. I could not deal with so much information. The past seemed more accurate than what I have been doing in the past sixteen months, and only Aisling memory was branded in my soul with fire I would never erase.

I was not afraid of the future. It is the past that is consumed me. It may happen that the people we loved miss them more than those who loved us. I comprehend that the desire to love and the search for meaning are more overpowering than the desire to be loved. How many times I found myself feeling happy but with tears in my eyes.

I told Carol every ray of sunshine, every drop of rain I traveled through during the past 18 months. After so much, I finally understood that we do not begin to live life when we think we have achieved everything; every one of us begins to live life when we have something missing or taken from us. I had to lose myself or lose what I thought to be me to find myself.

She told me she felt betrayed. Stabbed at her chest, but there was no knife to pull out. She and others did not comprehend why I would vanish without a word or explanation. To think of the worst was the only thing left. While talking, she had a sweet expression of alleviation, relief, and comfort, something it would make me trust my life on her. When Carol asked me impatiently, "And what now?" I didn't know what to say.

Only I could determine how long I needed to walk in hell until finding peace. It was like seeing myself and losing the essence of myself at the same time. In a way, my life was coming to an end, and at the same time, I was recovering memories one by one slowly, gently. Carol did not agree to let me return to my hotel. She insisted that I come with her; she would not let me walk away.

Nothing quite brought out the passion for life in me, like the thought of the impending death of my life with a lost identity. I wanted to write all my fears, my doubts, and conflicting ideas on a big piece of ice and wait for the sun to see them all vanish.

The death of a dream can, in fact, be the starting point for even a bigger one. I heard the sound of Aisling humming my name. I am sure she would share my happiness.

The last hours brought several highly diverse sentiments in me. First, the confusion, after acknowledging the facts, the healing time, and finally, my heart started to shine an old light buried deep inside.

Listening, clinging to a person that knew more about me than myself, was not a choice. During the following days, we visited every place she wanted. We met people that I did not know at all, but they knew the old me. Some memories and faces were returning; others were still strangers. Many real moments disappeared from my life, and I did not have the memories to bring them back.

Days went by one at a time. One early morning Carol decided to bring back more memories. She took me to my house. As with the business, she was the person I had given the legal power to administer my belongings in an emergency. Entering a place where all your yesterdays were buried is bizarre. She apologized because they started unfurnishing the site a couple of weeks ago; it was not reasonable to keep the maintenance cost if nobody was using it. Carol objected to letting people use the house; somehow, it did not seem right. Being in a home that you did not remember is like walking through darkness with only flashes of yesterday. After all, I was home, but it felt as if getting closest to a destination was feeling to be the farthest away. I told Carol to continue disposing of all things in the house. There was no point, no future, in even trying to go back.

Sadness was in my yesterday. If, for a moment, I wished the beautiful fragrance of dreams to revive once again, I now concede that it is not obtainable to bring back the past. I am not the same man who lived in this house some time ago.

I told Carol about Aisling, how I have slept many nights crying on my pillow. How my soul feels incomplete without her in my life. How I keep finding the memories of the girl I unquestionably loved everywhere. I miss falling asleep listening to her heartbeats. Aisling is someone in my life whom I will miss always! Carol said, "She may be gone from your sight but be happy because she will never leave your heart."

There were so many days when I wished my memory to be less moody when I would have given anything to get in touch with a person with meaning in my world. Carol told me and about Sharleen. If I had had people sliding slowly from my mind, I think it would not hurt so much. It also must be sad to see someone not remembering you. I imagine Sharleen would love to talk about moments spent together, and I do not know if those memories will ever return.

At that moment, I had only Aisling in my heart. Her name was engraved with fire inside me, and nobody or nothing could ever occupy a place that was reserved for her.

Paradoxically I was going to meet Sharleen the next day. Carol had contacted her. Sharleen wanted to meet here in the city, the city we used to love, and lived together for more than three years. I made my soul understand already some time ago that we cannot have everything in life. I have discovered something I did not even have a name for. I did not think to know more or have any answers, but the experience taught me how to live and appreciate being alive. How could I explain that life was now asking for my life?

The morning was sunny, light-filled my room. I wished I could shine some of that light into my mind. Strangely as it may sound, I was not convinced of the good at meeting an old love. Someone with whom I decided to go separate ways. Perhaps she had never belonged to me; who, after all, belongs to whom.

For someone who was through the process of identifying himself and daily examining my memories, it was not convenient to forget the miracles that life had given me. Once I was desperately trying to remember, and now I was unsure. Now that I have recognized bits of memories, I was worried if I was better off not knowing.

We walked to a small coffee shop with Carol, one we visited many times before my crash. I saw an attractive woman standing outside, sauntering in our direction.

She had a nervous smile on her face. Sharleen moved her face toward mine, our foreheads nearly touching, and asked, "Is it really you?" Memories are heartbeats of the heart. I stared for an instant in Sharleen's eyes and saw part of my own heart. Memory has entrapped me again, like in a story, in flashes, a feeling aroused in me, which I was not expecting. I said, "Sharleen, I do not remember you, but my heart does." She hugged me and said, "I knew you were not dead; I never doubted, never."

That night tears were in my eyes. Tears I know not what they denote, but deep in my heart is where they originate. They do not ask for permission, nor I desire them to run to my eyes. That night I dreamed of long autumn nights, of long walks along the beach, of kisses under the moonlight, on things that will never be.

Not only my life had changed. It is beautiful to meet someone by chance and have this stranger invite us to live again. That is what happened with Sharleen. She would tell me. "I want to wither, looking at the same face every morning." Sharleen has a big heart. When a mistake was made, she always gave her partner more time than they deserve to correct it. For her, love was about seeing a person and accepting all their light and dark shades. It was never black or white. Talking to her was showing me how I was before today. If she did love me, I was not a horrible person, although knowing that I lost her also told me that I was not enough for her.

Tom, she said, "We had a beautiful time together, the best time I can remember, but when you have something special, it was crazier not to want to spend the rest of our life together, Tom, you never wanted that."

Carol had told me before that Sharleen had found someone new in her life. She did fall in love as I did. I guess hearts that had known love are always going to find love again in their lives.

She looked at my eyes but reached deep into my heart and, with a soft smile, said, "With Steve, as with you, we do not find fault with each other but accept each other as we are and forgive each other every day from the bottom of our hearts. The difference is now I have a future." She was looking at me with serene eyes and said. "That is what I wanted. I wanted to be someone's love forever."

Words do have a way to touch parts of you, details you do not remember you had. I took her hand and trying to show her that she was not a complete stranger and said, "In my darkest hour when I was alone, and not a single memory was there to speak words of comfort, some tiny flame in my heart kept burning so that I could find a way back. That flame must have been you. I thank you for that."

I had found and lost someone apparently because I was not ready for endless tomorrows in the limitlessness of space and the immensity of time. In the same vastness of time, I found and lost someone, believing in endless tomorrows.

Will the same day ever come back, when we can be feeling old joy, or does time take all away, never giving back our best days. Wishing to grab the old life with a few memories was not easy, but no matter where I was, Aisling's memory was intact, not like the half-forgotten life I had before.

Chapter XII

Science and religion.

I may have been driving too fast down winding roads without considering the risk for the people around me or me. To destroy is easy to arise from the ruins and do something better, not so much.

There is nothing more miraculous than science, where existence jumps out nothing. It goes against our beliefs, making the impossible turn possible. The safest way to obtain the unlikely is to disregard all notions of impossibles and reach out of madness for what we cannot achieve.

I wanted to defy logic to risk climbing to the edge of a precipice jump and hope for a miracle.

I express admiration for the scientific spirit. The willingness to try again after something has proven wrong, the knowledge but certainty of not knowing all.

At the hospital where they treat GBM, one of the most common and aggressive human brain malignancies, doctors advise me about a new drug. Many patients have benefited from this innovative drug delivery strategy, and they recommended I do the same. Local administration of medication to the brain has led to a significant improvement in survival rates, and at least my life expectancy would be longer.

In a situation like this, it is not uncommon to think about death and religion. So I do not believe I am convinced that God exists. It is unfounded, in my opinion, to claim that there is no God. It is as irrational or arrogant to allege that there is one. I firmly admit that there is nothing I do irrefutably know. I am committed to my willingness to embrace what is right rather than what feels good but never want to testify to be absolutely in possession of the truth.

Consistently, I see that the holy book of any religion in one man's hand is worse than a whiskey bottle. It can blind you to do the most horrifying deeds in the name of God. Those who can make you believe farcicalities can make you commit atrocities.

Whether or not you regard yourself to be a believer, I find God to be beneficial to us. We can see the immensity of the cosmos, and it is easy to get lost in this vast infinity. When we abandon our trust in a power greater than us, we leave behind our sense of responsibility.

On the other hand, I admire Atheism. Atheism is an attitude, a frame of mind that accurately looks at the world courageously, always trying to understand everything as part of existence.

For me, it is far better to apprehend the Universe as it is than to persist in delusion, however satisfying and reassuring that could be.

I value the way some people interpret life. They believe God allows us to experience the low points of life to impart lessons that we could master in no other way. Our belief can free us but also can chain us to false conclusions. I do not believe in absolutes in good and evil; I do not think you can threaten people into goodness.

I do not need a religion, no temples, no wishful expectations. To believe does not mean the death of intelligence. Simple is not less right. I want to follow my heart, for it affects everything else I do. I do not see a road in front of me; I am walking, not knowing where I go or what to expect. Trying to live in harmony with my heart and believing that I am doing right does not mean that I am doing so.

I wish to be the day and night. To go south and arrive in the north. To be all and nothing, to be the sun, moon, and only the wind. I want to be wish-free.

I will always believe in love. Love brought me pain and broke me down, but it was the experience of love that shape me the most.

I still look for you in all the faces, searching in all the places you have never been to before. How tenderly I would smile to you though you would not smile in return. I yearn to look into your eyes, though they will no longer have a ray of recognition for me. I wish to win your heart though hearts do not beat for me anymore.

I asked myself a question, one I had to reply to with two distinct answers. Every new inquiry raised more challenges. I tried only to replay, giving one solution, but every question creates more interrogations. I am facing an impossible task. Acceptance is an attitude we should not underestimate. I started to accept whatever situation I was experiencing, focusing on how to get the best of anything life throws at me. It made me realize that embracing what is in front of me helped me become a much more content person.

Acceptance should be completely voluntary, not compulsory.

Our greatest dreams could become a reality in the future. With the advances in technology at our disposal, the possibilities are unlimited. We ought to create a more just world, reduce the gap between rich and poor, accept each other, not destroy the world we are lucky to have inherited.

After Carol explained what my job was before the airplane accident, life was tough to absorb. I was neither the old nor the new me. There is nothing rarer than to be torn between two worlds claiming to be both yours. My memory was returning only in fragments. To let my mind dissuade me from my dreams was not the future I was looking to establish. I do not want to let pride go to my head and gloom my heart. I know what feels hollow better than many, and I appreciate every hand offered to me.

Acknowledging my health situation and my mind's incompleteness, I decided to withdraw from my company's old position. I sold the business to Carol and my other ex-employees. It is always important to know when a phase in your life has reached its end. I am leaving my past without negating its validity or its former importance in my life.

Nevertheless, I can believe how fast time goes by. I woke up today to find that my life has rushed by at light speed. So many intense moments occurred only yesterday. The pain of losing Aisling is the only consistent pain not touched by time; I still miss her lips that do not smile anymore. Her departure reminds me that no caress will ever feel the same again because no other girl will ever be like her.

Following the expectations of my doctors, I should have between 4 and 6 months to live. The headaches are with the help of medicaments under relative control. Now I have to decide how and when to die. First, I will sign a living will. A "living will" is a legal certificate that lets people state their wishes for end-of-life medical care. Without a legal document expressing those wishes, family members and doctors can only speculate what a gravely ill person would prefer in terms of treatment. It also enunciates other vital questions, detailing your tube feeding preferences, artificial hydration, etc. A living will becomes applicable only when you cannot communicate your desires on your own.

My eyes will be heartily welcome the long sleep, the sleep without dreams, a warm blackness to erase everything else.

Aisling, when I take my last breath, I will think of you, and if there is a bridge to cross, I will be waiting for you to be there to help me get onto the other side. I know that I will never love less, that I will never forget that you will constantly be with me.

The how-to die portion of my death is possible to control. We must be willing to accept that it is not the number of hours you live what counts but how you live and what you do with the time at your disposal. I will travel to Switzerland short before the time is near. Swiss law since 1937 permits assisted suicide by anyone for altruistic reasons. Only our misplaced apprehension for the doctrine of human life's sanctity prevents us from acting in a humanitarian way. I demand freedom of choosing when to die.

Euthanasia is Greek for "easy death," and it is true; there is no more painless death than this. Sadly, people are so afraid of death in all its forms that they find it so strenuous even when death should be peaceful.

Impossible turning possible should be ordinary, and miracles should not become the only hope in the darkness of the places I had fallen lately. Science could also be the light taking me out of the hopelessness of my condition. Every discovery was giving me more hope, more time.

After everything I have been through and what had to happen to people, I loved, being here is part of a miracle I should value and recognize.

I effused my fear of death by concentrating on reaching the dreams of others. Loving the memories of Aisling was like a commitment to forever, and although the human touch was missing, I was not giving up expectations to find love on earth.

Life had decided that Aisling and I should not walk the same road hand in hand anymore. My heart had decided never to forget, and my hands missed the warmth of her hands. My eyes searched for her continually, but I could not see her. I did not know if to trust my heart that told me she was always nearby or my eyes that could not see her. I wished to say to her, "Aisling, I am right beside you, and I will love you always."

I used to keep it a long distance from hospitals, but they are often on my schedule, and I am in the hands of the hospital staff one more day. My brain is firing off messages telling me to run away and forget all about treatments. How many hours and days are worth investing in the cure if the gain could be less the time invested?

The artificial light emanating from spotlights in the ceiling and the reassuring smell of antiseptic was another fact furiously trying to make run away. Outside, the sun was shining, birds were singing, trees were swaying with the southern wind, so many reasons to wish not to be there.

Only the left hemisphere of my brain kept me waiting there for a scientific judgment. There was in that room unquestionably an underlying confusion in my senses and my expectations.

When the negative drowsiness of waiting tried to get me to sleep, my doctor opened the door. He looked me in the eyes and said. "I am not gonna give you the illusionary news but decidedly good news." A revelation of hope made me wish he would resume explaining, so I beg him to continue. "According to the measurement taken that day, it was reasonable to expect extending my life expectancy for at least one or an even longer time," he encouragingly said.

I was not sure what to believe, but I said pointedly, "You gave me the strength I needed. I am more than happy to have some hope available, thank you.."

That evening I wanted to share the news of an extra year of life expectancy with someone. Naturally, I called Carol, who agreed to meet, and she called Sharleen to see if she could join us. Friendship marks life in a more profound way than we would assume. If something important is not shared, it somehow loses the unique taste that makes it essential.

The first sentence Carol said was the reflection of her soul. She embraced me, saying, "Life is so endlessly delicious. I am so happy." After a short sigh, she said, "Your mind must be bare if you dare to think that you can leave us more than once."

While we talked, waiting for Sharleen, she called, explaining that it was impossible to meet that night. She sent her love and apologies for not making it.

It was a pleasant evening, and it did not matter what we spoke. All that was necessary was to see a friend sharing, even if it was with only a smile.

When we fully understand the brevity of life, every second is a gift you hold dear. Every second brings you closer to the person sharing that fleeting moment.

I loved the simplicity of Carol. For her, it was important not to elaborate too much on a subject. She was open and always had a straight answer to your questions. When I asked how she managed to stay so focused, she only replied, "Find your heart, and you will find your way to act." She stood motionless and focused for a short while before she said, "I give best when I give from my heart."

There was so much we wanted to talk about but time passed too fast and soon was late. I had to tell Carol how happy I was to have her as a friend. I had to tell her how much I valued her way of interpreting life and her incredible profound insight into reality. She was a true friend, one I was lucky to have back in my memories.

By that time, I was not staying at her house anymore. I had rented a small flat in the city. The rent was a little lower in Croatia than in Ireland, so I was satisfied with my new home.

Carol had come by car that evening, so we went outside. It was a calm night; a gentle breeze from the ocean reminded me of older days. I brought her to the car, and we said good night.

I was delighted that she came. I was really in use of someone else's smile that night. Carol was a beautiful and glamorous woman with a great heart but with a disastrous quality in choosing the wrong man in her sentimental life. We did talk about that night, and it made me sad to see her disappointed in man. Talking about her personal life, I felt a distance that she wanted to keep. There was a line that she did not want to cross but in her sharing was sadness. She could not selectively numb her anger, and I could not find the words to avoid her feeling that way.

I knew she treated her employees as equals and with honesty. She was a fair and gentle person. I prayed for better days, but nothing is certain. I was not worried about Carol running her business; my concern was her choosing solitude to avoid breaking her heart into pieces. Nothing would ever have pleased me more than to see her finding a loving partner.

Chapter XIII


Promoting art.


I t is noble to spend time searching for the meaning of life, but if the time is confirmed to be limited, taking some action is crucial and more imperative than finding the purpose. We would never see the answer by ourselves; we find it with each other.

Through the relentless succession of moments during which I confront myself with the urgency of deciding what steps to take next, every project presented a range of exciting possibilities. Finally, after much deliberation, I set my mind to help artist promote their creations.

Art is losing yourself, creating something that, after finishing, helps to find the creator. Art always serves beauty. An artist must look and express what he sees deep inside, not minding if they are unsure of what is seeing. A compositor, writer, or artist cannot expect to be glorified by people. It is unnecessary to reach millions; it is just enough that some hear a song, read a book, or appreciate a new handmade object. She or he does it because they have to because it is their vocation. Art is an expression of love.

The life of an artist can be harsh. It is not easy to make a living. My goal is to help create market opportunities for those using their talent, hobby, or profession. I have experienced the long hours Sharleen used to invest in creating something sublime for this world. The mystery of art resides in the relationship between the artist and their work. Often after working days, she would destroy a painting because she did not identify entirely with the end product; somewhat, only she would understand.

Through life, you create connections with people, and that links are energy waiting for action. Your ideas will be transformed into reality with your contacts' help if others can see and understand your task.

Of course, the first person I wanted to introduce this project was Sharleen.

Around 80 percent of the world's population has already had a deja-vu experience. According to scientists, it describes the phenomenon that leads us to believe that we have already lived through a moment. However, only a few know that there is also a counterpart to it call the jamais-vu. Now, jamais-vu is a sudden feeling of strangeness concerning events, people, or objects close to you. Being with Sharleen was very much like this. She remembers everything about our time together, but for me, most memories will never come back. Everybody is always a stranger.

It is effortless for me to get confused with my own life. I could easily refer to my existence as a story about absence and loss. Here I was three feet apart from Sharleen, looking into her eyes filled with old memories while I was fighting with uncertainties of first encounters.

"I am not a stranger," she said, feeling the confusion in me. For a split instant, we stared at each other, not knowing if to kiss or run away.

Sharleen, the girl with the sweetest smile and the easy ways, the girl I used to spend my days and nights with for so long. I knew she was social, amiable, and a gentle soul that time ago walked beside my side. An overwhelming curiosity forced me to ask her about us. I wanted to know about memorable times, things she regrets, hopes, and her current dreams.

She told me about our yesterdays, and time went by without us noticing that the sunlight turned to moonlight. I also wonder about you, Tom, Sharleen said suddenly at the end of silence, "Maybe it is if we go back to being strangers that would let us know we were never lovers in the first place." From strangers to lovers and lovers to strangers again, I did not want that to be our end. While letting my eyes wander all over her, I told her, 'I do not wish to end up being unknown to you who have known me for so long." I want to know you again; I will let my memories only be a murmur in a shady past. I have awkwardness in conceiving how it can be that you have some affection for me, but as you have, so I will try to be a light in your life. We had a beautiful time. At goodbye, I gave her a soft, whispered kiss promising her to be her friend every way I could.

I have always believed, and I hope I am not mistaken, that whatever comes negative or positive, we can always make sense of it and revert negativity into something positive. If a relationship breaks apart, both or at least one did not want to get over the problem and continue. No matter the crime, forgiveness is always possible.

The God that punishes for an eternity for the crimes of a split moment can never be my God. That would make him the cruelest, most selfish of creatures.

That night, we agreed to do the first market and art exposition in Bologna, where she has many other artists willing to use an opportunity like this. Yes, I am a dreamer and always hoping for the best. Despite seeming too optimistic, I think that even if we learn that not everything works as planned, we have an essential role in making things work.

I am fully aware of how difficult it is to get people to trust you, primarily if their living depends on selling enough to cover the expenses and gain money for subsistence.

With Sharleen, we agree to rent a hall in The Bologna Exhibition Center. The venue has 18 galleries, fully wired, air-conditioned, and equipped with state-of-the-art IT systems, where multiple events can be held thanks to 5 separate entrances simultaneously. Always the spot you select must conform with the best infrastructure your money can afford; if not, things get complicated even before you start. This site provides flexibility and mobility in affluence. A total of 14,500 covered parking spaces are at your disposal. Vehicle owners can reserve their space in advance.

To organize a big event and be successful many factors should be at your disposal. It would be best if you had time but time was not on my list. To counterbalance the short time available, I invested heavily in publicity. My strong representation through Sharleen allowed me to make contact with well-established artists around Europe. Once you get a couple of names to be mention things, sometimes go more smoothly.

Another person I asked for help with was Carol. She unveiled to me that there was another world where friends helped friends for no other reason than that it is good to do so. From the first minute, she was eager to help in every possible way. Charlotte heard about this enterprise and offered sponsorship for some events. Suddenly, this at start scarry dream seemed to be growing on his own; it was stranger than fiction to me.

Recognizing that the difference between a successful and unsuccessful business is how well participants can "bond" during the organizing period is fundamental to any project. I reserved an extended portion of my time talking to everyone working through these weeks, no matter their position. Why is it always that we do not regret the things we have done right but only the things left undone? The stuff we craved to do and never did. For this one event, I was giving all, never considering the risk. Somehow I thought I had nothing to lose.

The idea of "Having nothing to lose" kept spinning in my head for a time until I remembered my loved Aisling. One day during our regular walks through the streets of Limerick, she said that she was afraid of losing me. When I asked if she had doubts about my feelings for her, she said, "No, you silly, it has nothing to do with doubt. It means that if I am not a little afraid of losing you, it would mean that I do not love you right."

So I had to reconsider my attitude and recognize that having nothing to lose does not make you stronger but weaker. The more is at risk, the more you need to find the strength to succeed.

It was a touching moment meeting with Charlotte again. I was so indebted to everything she had done for me. She was one of the people responsible for all the good in my new life.

Charlotte told me one afternoon when she came to reconnect with someone who came into her life with no warnings and left with no past, "You are sort of dangerous, you know?" I stared at her. "Me?"

She smiled and said, "I am way too honest with you." Charlotte was an intelligent woman that appreciated art and understood the need of hard-working people. She would tell me later, "The ripples of the generous heart are the essential blessings of the universe."

Weeks went by, and the final weekend was just days away. Sharleen was spending more time with me, and during the evening, we always found the opportunity to exchange words. We both had that feeling that our life could have been another, different, better in a way impossible to utter. Now because I had only a few broken fragments of memories, she would never get the chance to return to the person she was once in love time ago. She regretted making some decisions; somewhere along the way was another road we missed.

Late I was learning that I must never live my life being concerned about my happiness alone but always in the happening which is going on around me. Working with people is still notoriously exhausting. You do not archive connections between persons by tie one to another. It demands understanding and communication.
Bring minds, hearts, and souls together, and you will strengthen relationships.

Days passed one by one, each bringing their troubles, anecdotes, and surprises. Each day I knew more about the world than I knew the day before; each day, there was something else I wanted to do, eyes that vainly crave the light of thousand tomorrows.

I wanted to sit there, not to talk, not worrying, only contemplating existence passing by. For a long time, I had been too busy, and I wanted not to listen to others. I wanted to enjoy the silence before the storm. In a little, while it would be different. Soon it would be tomorrow, the opening day of our first "International Art Expression Day." The event is a three-day opportunity to present to numerous people creations of different areas of art. The official ceremony is starting at 11:00 on Friday.

Like almost every evening during the last few weeks, Sharleen came to spend evening hours with me. Tonight we did not talk about work. We both understood that the future mattered not at all. We had done our job the best way we could. Now it was the time to let things go their way, trusting that our efforts would bring the expected results.

I said, "There are things I need to tell you, Sharleen, "Do you care to join me for a walk?" She gave him one broad smile and said, "A moonlight stroll with you? Do you even have to ask?"
Along the streets, as we did while living together, we walked hand in hand. Over our heads, the light of a moon barely illuminated anything. We knew our time together was in the past, but love was still around if we let ourselves believe such a thing is possible. Sharleen said, "I will spend my life believing in you."
I loved the notion that we had time to spend together. I love us together this way, just like this. To Sharleen, the slightest misuse of words would bring back some old wounds that never truly healed. I was unaware of the things I did in the past but could notice some sadness in her eyes after expressing my thoughts. Pain is a sudden hurt that you cannot avoid taking over you, and there is nothing you can do to stop it.

Sharleen confessed that her relationship was over, not because of me but because she knew it was more she needed. She had this urgent wish to believe that falling in love is easy. Falling in love with the same person was destiny. I never wanted to talk about my medical condition, but I could not bear hiding this from her.
The words we say when we speak never decipher into precisely what we mean. After I told Sharleen it was a prolonged silence, then silently, she asked, "How long." I

told her that it was uncertain that the new drug was working, but it was impossible to know.

Then she softly put her hands on either side of my face and kissed me feelingly; I do not recollect ever getting so lost in a kiss before. I paused, leaning over to lay my lips on hers, and told myself, "It's time to feel again."

We kissed passionately for all the lost time we were apart. Sharleen whispered in my ear, "Only to know that you have more than one day is all I need."

It was good to be in her arms, and for her, it was good to be in mine; nothing good is truly lost.

Every word she ever spoke came effortlessly from her heart. She would tell friends, "Months I lived in love, followed by months full of pain and heartache. Those are the times that defined me."

There is a thin line dividing laughter and pain. The more you love, the more you let yourself left open to pain and sorrow. Sharleen always wanted to be someone's heart, even if that desire meant breaking her own.

That Friday morning, I woke up with Sharleen in my arms. I look at her, and with our faces turned fully to face each other, we made a promise to love each other for the sake of love alone. I do not know what she sees in me, but I see eyes of surpassing tenderness and calm beauty of a girl that deserved to be loved.

I shivered at the sight of her lovely face, longing to keep that tender smile smiling at me, haunting me, driving me mad.

That singular Friday was our day, and we would fight to make things happen. Maybe the word "fight" is not adequate. I want to symbolize the drive inside us to create hope, a light in what will always be a very harsh world.

Not hoping for anything will destroy you for sure and extinguish imagining a world worth living in tomorrow.

As strangely it may sound, I believe that we sometimes fight each other while dreaming of the same things.

The secret to achieving a goal is personal dedication, entirely giving the best of you. The side effect will be mostly succeeding in your endeavor.

It was comforting to walk alongside visitors, passing through the different stands where the artist exposed their work. How beautiful it is to be standing next to a stranger, gazing at the same object that caught our attention, an unspoken passion between us.

When all was over, Sharleen was exhausted, craving for a quiet place where she could reflect on our achievement. She said, "Win or lose, we are trying; that is what preponderates."

Unwillingly faded into the shadows of my mind. Trying with tears in my eyes to bring back the moments shared long but not so long ago. And kissing desperately the lips of the girl I had in front of me so that this memory could never fade again was how I spent every day since the first night saw us falling to sleep in each other's arms.

Sharleen said softly into my ear, believing I was already sleeping, "Let the deadly love of my life go on. You escaped me once, leaving only misery and pain behind every corner of my soul. You are planning to leave me again no matter how much this woman needs you. You ask for all of me, and I will give all of me because I am yours and do not know how to avoid it."

## Chapter XIV

Trough Sharleen's eyes.

I s it possible to love someone so unselfishly that knowing it would hurt you and break you and finally erase you would not matter because it is the only thing you can do?

There was no repentance that I could have spoken. There was no crime I was charged with other than disappearing without a word. No insurance policy has ever been devised to protect for a case like this. Maybe I was accused of a crime I did not commit. I was not charged formally but by default. The only cure for the suffering that people went through was to listen to their words. Each told me the same story but with different approaches and different interpretations of the same truth. I had my version, and it was a sad, lonely one. One I was still living, one where my demons were still torturing my soul.

We want amnesty from the accusations. To free ourselves from the pain of having done wrong. It was not important if I was guilty or not; nobody was looking to punish me. It was the knowledge of the pain we caused willingly or not.

I had stumbled my way through reality since the day I return from nothingness. There was always the hope of having people who loved me before I did lose all memories. By the time I had recovered some recollections and had someone loving me, I also started to ask myself another dreadful question.

What could I say to Aisling to earn her forgiveness?

People are allowed to be screwed up, fall, do terrible things, and hope to find a way out of misery.

Nothing should stay out of forgiveness; we must let the darkness wash away from our souls so that we stand in the light of the sun again.

Realizing that sharing the feelings deep in our hearts is not an illusion finally liberates us from seeking redemption of unearned guilt.

One night we were lying in bed talking about things we would like to do. Sharleen, smiling, started telling me excitedly about the book she was reading now. There is this theory the author is trying to make us understand; she would say to me, "He believes that if you live in a dark place and an unexpected light shines for a short time, people will be in deeper darkness after the light goes out." Sharleen looked at me with a sad expression on her face and continued saying: I think it is the absolute truth. Before I met you, I was alone, but after you came into my life and left me, I felt so much more isolated, so much more alone. After that night at the harbor, I wanted to die. I felt betrayed by someone I have given all I had, thinking I am a nobody, I am no good enough, rejected, and abandoned. Just for a moment, I ponder that I might never see you again, and that felt worse than death. I wanted to run after you. I know that I could have convinced you to stay with me. I wanted to beg you; please let us always stay together, so I can at least see you.

Tom, be so kind as to understand that it was one of those times you feel a sense of loss no matter what way you go. Part of me knew I did not have you in the first place. I guess that is what frustration is. To realize losing someone that you may have never had. I knew it in my heart. That this time our separation was final. I had irrevocably made my choice, and so had you. You let me go. Part of me was relieved because I was doing the best for my sanity, making the right decision. What I did not expect or foresee was to feel so much pain and grief. It felt final, but I always believed that we would find our way back to each other every time again and again. We would stay connected by all the little things that we felt for each other no matter what.

When Carol called me asking if I knew from you, I did not understand. Why would she not know where you were? I missed you like hell; I hated you for leaving me alone and lonely. Have you ever departed from someone you love and wanted one more chance to discuss ways to continue, one more opportunity to reconsider the options? One more day to bring back all the times we promise us forever?

Carol knew that your escape was work. She was hoping to find you with me. We never accepted the idea of you just running away from us, of you disappearing.

It is useless for me to portray how terrible we felt all the time that followed your disappearance. You not only took all the little hopes I had but sentenced me to accept complete defeat. The last thing you lose or let go of are your expectations. You disappearing took even the last of the lights shining the tiniest of lights in me.

Carol came to Bologna, and we checked all possible places asking for you. If you have ever lost someone essential to you, you already know how it feels, and if you have not, you cannot possibly imagine it. I also speak for Carol when I said that you vanished from us, leaving behind a feeling of immeasurable emptiness.

Some lonely night at Carol's hotel, we were crying together. She said to me, "I cannot say goodbye." Carol was crying, and somewhere inside me, I was crying, too, because I felt unavoidable things at last. I was experiencing not just the physical pain but all that I have lost, and it is a profound and catastrophic regret of not having done nothing that will leave an abyss in me that nothing would ever fill.

It is the shallowness of the encouragements that cause the trouble.
"You'll get over it...", "In time, they tell me, I would not feel so bad." Friends and strangers, everyone kept telling me that time heals all wounds, but no one could tell me what I needed, what I was supposed to do at that moment. Losing you and knowing that your life went on would not hurt me as it was not knowing where you were, not knowing if you were well. After days Carol returned to Croatia; there was nothing else we could do. So many days, I did not know if I wanted to hate you or die for you.
The spaces between the times thinking of you and missing you grow longer. Memories of you kept stabbing pain to my heart. Sometimes I wanted to believe it is of no use to love. Lovers only go out of your life and leave a more abysmally hurt than the emptiness before they came.

More than a year went by, and I needed love to be alive again. You were gone. I could not remember when I had been laughing effortlessly since then. I needed to accept and live again. I asked God to help me get over you and find new love, but I do not decide how the miracle will occur. Just watch for the signs.

One morning while working on a new painting, the phone rang. It was Carol; she wanted to know about me, about my days, about how I was doing. We spoke for a few minutes, but I always had the suspicion that she was calling for something more. After a short silence, she said,

"He is back...but." But it was the part that I was afraid to hear. I begged her to please explain the "but."

I never wanted to resume that painting, and as for today, you will always find that it is unfinished.

In the night of my heart, it is like the dawn gave space to dreams again. My heart rebuilt with hope, resurrected illusions killed by pain and hurt were letting me smile too. Now my world was no longer confused in the obsession with darkness. There's been a death of sorts, but no resurrection is possible without a few eons in hell. That day I knew miracles exist and decided that I will look for you in every lifetime and love you there.

Now, Tom, you know what you did to me, I will not let you die do you hear me?

I expected myself to say something. I felt like I were in someplace my body cannot sense, and panic at having to speak stole the thoughts from my head. Later I became conscious, and without paying attention to words, I embraced her and said, "My love, I will not only die for you, but I also want to live for you."

We both accepted the risk of being hurt. W knew that the most important thing was that we were together. Eventually, one of us was going to get hurt again. Life would not stop bringing happiness, and happiness reflects the sadness in the mirror of time.

There is a time in life when you expect the world to be always smiling at you. Silence can be breathing space between the many words interchanged during the day or an open the door to new communication methods. We should not let silence be a lack of connection to be the end of togetherness. So it is our right to expect an eternal smile in the face of the world, but we also have to make it possible.

When rivers of emotions break the defenses, let me be the one holding your hand and help to calm the burst of your beating heart. I believe in loving you every day more and more. Does it mean I did not love you enough yesterday? Presence and absence are essential to keep us going. We need the silence to speak the right words; we need the lack of ourselves to be present when it matters most.

With Aisling gone, time seemed to have frozen. With Sharleen, time was a constant reminder of the end rushing towards us. Every night before going to sleep, I stared at her face wishing to keep the passing of the seconds engraved on my mind so that I can rewind all as many times as I wanted. I needed her skin touching mine. I needed to be close entangled with her, not to know where she ended, and I began.

There was no wind that night as if the dark sky was holding breath and the stars were only shining for us. Sharleen left the book aside and put her arms around me. Through the open window, we starred at the not quite full moon and wondered about the many more surprises life had waiting for us. The moon looked down, needing admiration in our eyes.

I knew how strong Sharleen was. I knew she did not want to think of the little time we had to spend together. In a way, she was in denial. How can you blame someone for escaping reality? For closing her eyes and avoid dealing with the fact that the future without me was inevitable. Always and in every always, the absence was closer. Our love was more sound than before, mainly because I had changed, mainly because her passion did not change, mostly because time took eternity away from us.

There in the quiet, there was a kind of hush, the sort of silence that bonded us. Sharleen whispered into my ear, "Tonight, it is not about you. It is about how your absence troubled me and will trouble me again. While the moon watches over us, my thoughts ask how to keep you forever in my memory. It is not about how to say goodbye; it is how never to let you go." I was holding her head on my chest. Feeling one tear roll out and touch my heart. For me, it was on how to hide all of this hurt, feeling incapacitated to alter my condition, paralyzed by my human nature.

I looked at myself with Sharleen's eyes. I knew the pain inside her because I had experienced too well losing Aisling. There were no words I could have said. The pain is yours, and you alone must deal with it. I felt I only had kisses and caresses with all the tender sounds of silence to distract her from the pain she knew was coming. While our bodies melted together and time allowed us to feel infinity, we fell asleep dreaming of never-ending sunsets.

Chapter XV

Golden days.

There was something strange in my awareness, something indescribably sweet. The thought of days with Sharleen, at that moment, encouraged and delighted me like wine. Was it possible to love too much? I wanted to love her passionately. Wishes can come true if the desire is strong enough. I was willing to risk failure anything resulting from this wish of giving all of me to love her. My mind must be delusional if I would dare to think I can love more than now.

Strangely that morning, I did not hear Sharleen getting up. When I went down to her studio, I found her finishing a new painting. Her face lit up, and she smiled gently. Come, Tom, keep moving; we must never stop. Let us continue our revolution! I took her in my arms, promising never to let go. We wished for butterfly kisses and to touch the stars, dreams too dearly to sell them, too lovely to let them go.

It was time to think about what to do next. We wanted to sleep out alone under the stars, conquer new worlds, to live our dreams.

If our forever was ending tomorrow, how would this reflect in our today? The aspiration is to enjoy life and cause motivation for others. Not letting days pass away, waiting for better ones ahead. We were happy to have more time but we could not stop the tide of life receding slowly in front of our eyes.

The result of our "Exposition" was stimulating and give us the strange comfort in knowing that no matter what we do next, we could succeed. The struggles we endure today will be the "good old days" of tomorrow.

We agree to shower, get ready, and walk to the center to meet with Carol, who wanted to introduce us to a new idea she developed while visiting our event. I did not need to know how much longer my life was going to be. The only thing I was sure of is that I wanted to enjoy life with the woman whom I loved all the days of my fleeting life. Taking the long way to the park and through the market, we slowed our pace down as we did while strolling along the beach. Sharleen always took the time to talk about the past. If some memories had left my consciousness, she patiently wished me to recollect the good times we had, repeating the events again and with all the details so that I would know about all the lost past. She was never tired to recall our yesterdays. Sometimes she would say, "What you believe to be possible will always be." I think she may be right. Why should we have the capacity of imagination if it is not for making ideas real?

Because hope came from inside us, the world was a blank canvas ready to reveal the magic of a vision.

Carol was waiting at a cozy coffee shop with Charlie to comment about her plans. Like always, she had selected a charming place; great cappuccino and delicious morning pastries. It was never a business meeting with Sharleen and Carol sitting at the table. I take a moment to stop and look around me. And smile inside.

Charlie was a young computer visioner. Together with his team, they developed an exciting idea for artists to offer their products online—an online market for artists only.

That morning we could say that everything started as nothing. As expected, Sharleen was fascinated with the prospects of providing a source of income to multiple professionals and amateurs working exclusively with handmade products. The significant difference between available sites offering such feasibility is that we wanted to connect both worlds. To explain it most thoroughly is to know that this site will have a physical shop where people and artists could expose, store, and sell creations in as many cities as possible.

It was a massive project we could not bring alone into life. So we departed, hoping to meet again and study the prospects of successfully realizing it with more attention.

Sharleen was very enthusiastic about this idea, but I could see the fear of not having the time to see the results in her eyes. I would say more precisely; she was afraid I would not have the time for such an enterprise. I told her, "This afternoon, we can pretend I am taking you somewhere astounding, somewhere you have always wanted to go." She strangely looked at me and said, "I do not wish to pretend. Let us go there!"

We drove to Desenzano del Garda, a place we wanted to visit for a long time. Desenzano is the largest urban area on the lake and far less dominated by tourism than the neighboring tows. Around the harbor and in the old town, beautifully restored trading houses testify to Desenzano's long tradition as one of the most important trading centers in Northern Italy. After finding a small quiet place, we decided to explore the surroundings.

While walking, we discuss Carol's proposition. We have to pinpoint that there cannot be a successful enterprise unless there is a commitment unless primary factors work together like persistence and dedication. Sharleen was worried we would spend too much time working, sacrificing time together, time we did not have. There is always another tomorrow to do somewhat differently to do something where we could be closer. Will we seek new challenges at some not distant time, or will this be our last commitment?

Without dreams, I have to be content with living day after day with no expectations. I know how intensely Sharleen wants to make a difference for others and herself. To love is to accept a person entirely. I did not wish Sharleen to change how she felt about helping fellow artists; I did not want her to stop her revolution.

It will be demanding, but this project could be the vessel that contains both shelter and adventure for unnumerable souls.

Noticing that I have been in silence for some time, I hold Sharleen's hand and said to her, "There is not only one way, but there is also a scarcity of good projects." Let us make our steps clear to work together, remembering that we can make this happen. Sharleen looked back at me, at my eyes, and smiled, "This is who you are; these decisions took you here to this day. I would do anything to stay with you because I always loved you".

We decided to celebrate, focusing our attention on the transcendent meaning of our choices. Who in this world can say if we will be here tomorrow? The fears of losing me too soon torn Sharleen's hopes, but she never brought the topic into our conversation. If we decided to do this, we knew never to fear waking up again the next day, having nothing to celebrate in our hearts.

To Carol, our allegiance to the plan was not a surprise. She knew the willingness in us to stay the course with undivided intensity. After completing the legal details, we met to celebrate one more time. I got used to celebrating more and more; for me, every new day was a reason to celebrate. There are so many faults in our lives, but instead of focusing solely on our mistakes, we should appreciate every positive deed made.

Sharleen and I, we know each other. I know her and so myself, but I am not sure if I ever have learned all about myself. I can deny and avoid the truth. But I cannot destroy the effect of my actions. I must comprehend that love will always uncover the truth.

Before we returned, we wanted to spend more nights in unfamiliar places, with strangers and doing simple things. Sharleen told me many times, "Tom, you are crazy." I would always agree with her and say, "I know you think I am crazy; I would never deny such. I am crazy about my life with you about this moment, but mostly about you."

With Sharleen, I never experienced awkward silences. Some mysterious force would let us communicate without words. She would tell me that once we found back to each other in a long and silent embrace after fighting over some unmemorable something. Fights I would gladly let fade from my memory, but I would gladly keep good times folded in the deeps of my mind.

How is it that one day life is tranquil and you are happy, a little convinced that all is under control, and suddenly tragedy streaks again? It happened to me on various occasions. How can I prevent it from happening again? The answer is, "I cannot."

When dreadful things keep happening, you know you are alive.

Tragedy shows us the most genuinely inner self, and if we have learned something until that moment, the path to follow will be self-evident to us.

On the other side, if delightful moments are part of your life, what are they teaching you? Beautiful things there are at every step you take. Learn to notice them, look at the grass, the flowers, the tress, the moon, and the stars. Tragedy matters not to who has seen delight.

I had to return to the hospital for control, but Sharleen was walking by my side this time. Few joys can equal the mere presence of whom you value and love utterly. Nothing in the world is changeless, and we would be foolish asking anything to last. The real problem is that we are never ready for transcendental changes when they come. Now, after six months, I was back to the same place where they told me that I would probably live only six more months.

A curious sense of peace invaded me as I waited for the results of my test. Knowing that Sharleen was with me was more vital than any treatment available in the universe.

For Sharleen to take things peacefully would have been to change her nature. She wanted only and only one outcome.

We enter the doctor's office. He was looking apologetic, but in his face were no signs denouncing awful news. He spoke briefly and went direct to the point. The mass in my brain has reduced his size, and that was fantastic news, but he admitted that it was too soon to expect miracles. For now, I could continue taking the same treatment hoping that things would not reverse.

At that instant, we were only two lovers holding hands and in a hurry to reach the car. Always in some confusion, kissing again, carefully at first, studying the shape and texture of each other's lips and soon more fiercely trying not to let the moment escape us anew. My mind was utterly powerless. The fear of the luxury of having more time was welcome, and nothing could shatter the feeling growing in my soul.

Wishes and hopes are the most fragile things; one day, all is great the subsequent is dissolution. My wish must be specific and powerful enough to use my will to make it come true. The only goal demanding all of me was to see my beloved girl smile. I wanted to keep that in mind to never deviate from that goal.

Consider the implications of wishing something else but the happiness of your loved one. No amount of riches will bring hearts together separated by roads heading ways apart. Beauty is when both want to love. Sometimes couples know it, and sometimes they do not.

That afternoon we did not go for our routinary stroll through streets searching for a new place to discover. We went home; we wanted to join together in light of a little more time on our hands. After the lights went out and the fire of our passion passed into a peaceful sleep, our bodies remained entangled until the next day.

We did not expect to be touch by angels or to believe we deserved more, and I see there our success because when you do not demand more, every second extra is a gift from heaven, not an unearned tragedy.

Before closing my eyes, I whisper, "I hope you will always have something to smile on each day of your life." She wanted to think of something meaningful to say, but our bodies were too committed to touching that only a brief I love you came out of her lips, and she fell asleep.

Chapter XVI

As days went by.

The limitings of our existence should be more conscious of our day-to-day actions. Once, I only wished for one more chance to tell Aisling how much she meant to me. Probably she knew that well, but her sudden departure from this world wrecked all of me. I madly wished to have one more day with her. Her heart did not get to hear me say, "I love you" one more time, and her lips would never be able to reply to the words I did not say.

I had forgotten how horrifying it could feel not to have the chance to tell what is in our hearts. That pain still consumes part of me because it was not so long gone. I never wanted to find myself in a position where my words had to be cut off like the wings of a butterfly to avoid them flying away into nothingness.

Darkness has a bad reputation. I like, especially at night, to walk into a room, close the curtains and sit on a comfortable armchair with the lights turned off.

In the stillness of that room, there in the darkness where everything around me turned to black, I find inspiration. As diluted as I can become, being one with darkness more, I feel part of it. I can concentrate on essential ideas, search for answers and find peace. I am the seeker in the night, able to detect the lesser light, the one I would not have noticed otherwise.

Today I take the time to let Sharleen know that I love her. In the morning, no matter how stressful and busy the day starts, I take one instant to tell her, "My heart lives inside yours. I'm forever and ever honestly in love with you." You are entitled to bring about a habit to keep the passion and awareness alive every day of your life together. Your consciousness must remember the wisdom of your own life.

We had several meetings during the following days.

Between work, we took time to talk about her personal life, and she commented on mine. Carol was a good friend, and I would remind her of how much she meant to me. She mentioned to me what Sharleen was saying to some of her artist friends, "With him, I feel that I am savvier than my truth." The truth was reciprocal; she made me feel like the person I wanted to be.

Sharing my last days with Carol and Sharleen was the best idea for a great time, no matter how long it could be. Carol filled the days with resolution and energy while Sharlee filled my days with imagination

and the power of creating wonders.

We were enjoying our days and convincingly our nights. "I wish you were an immortal," Sharleen whispered to me one night in our bed. I pressed her naked body against mine and told her, "If you can retain me in your heart, I will be with you always and forever. "Sweet dreams, sweetheart," I softly murmured in her ear, my arm still around her. "See you in my dreams.", she susurrated, and while softly kissing, she fell asleep in my arms.

Sharleen always had this hunger to love other people. It was something irreversible in her nature. People want a reward for what they do. A lover wants only to be in love, and that is the way she was.

Looking at my past was like looking at a rearview mirror, unveiling that my dreams were always much closer than they appeared at that time. I am happy I never gave up on my dreams.

Predominantly Sharleen gets up before me. She does not need many hours of sleep; her sleep is light, and the tiniest noise wakes her up. She did not enjoy cooking, but that morning she surprised me by preparing a fruitful breakfast: freshly squeezed orange juice, the most amazing pancakes under the sun, thick country bacon with eggs, and a bowl of frosted cereal, the best way to start one Sunday morning. Something there that sparked with warmth in her eyes was telling me more than words can say, so I told her, "Whatever you want from me, it is yours." She started laughing and said, "I want this day, all the hours and all the minutes in between, to spend them just you and me."

We did not set one foot out of the house that Sunday. It was a long kiss that, once it started, never really ended. We always had something to think about, talk about, and laugh and dream during those days. United hearts will not stop communicating in the silence between the cessation of words. It is peaceful, being there in the present, not having to do anything but enjoy the warmth of her body. I laid my head on Sharleen's shoulder and shut my eyes, invited toward sleep by the tender caress of fingers through my hair and her other palm against my cheek, light and warm as sunshine. I whispered, "I want the sound of your voice aimed at me. I want to consume the gleam of your eyes." At night, we fell asleep as lovers do, with angels secretly smiling and the silence of the night guiding our heartbeats.

On days when the world was spinning out of control, it was hard to find the time to chill, but we promised ourselves never to let work take our time away. Today we walked trying to discover new places, taking a sudden turn right or left to see something new and where to stop and have a coffee. It is hard to find a person who wants to walk the streets with me instead of rushing in a car.

It was a happy surprise to find Carol at our office. Usually, she always writes before coming. She had exciting news she wanted us to hear personally. Tom, Sharleen, said Carol, "I am getting married."
I wanted to congratulate her, but words failed me. The unique person she fell in love with, I had no idea who he was. We did not let Carol get out of the room before she would spill out all information and at least confess the name of the lucky man. She did not know him or his family very long, but she said, "Quickly, he convinced me that our passionate feelings were true." His name is Jordan.
We promise Carol to think about her and Jordan from today onwards as my best friends; she should count on our blessings. It makes me hopeful to see lovers reflect their joy in others. We go through life trying to be happy, but in the end, we must accept that happiness in its most natural sense is the unselfish ability to love other people.

Carol invited us to visit her. A sudden look at Sharleen's eyes, followed by her smile, was all I needed to see. I agree to go and spend the weekend in her city.
I love it when you do that, Sharleen whispered in my ear. She loved our silent communication, the way I read her eyes. She added, "I love the way your eyes gaze into mine; I feel a tender language of your heart, speaking to mine."
For an instant, I thought about a forest; every one of us is a tree growing beside another tress but all reaching for the same sunlight. You may see no connection at first

sight, but we are closely intertwined with each other deep under.

The daylight was slowly fading, the world's noises falling silent while our office's people were working long hours. Not often, we had to force ourselves to leave the building. A taxi was waiting for Carol to bring her to the airport. Before saying goodbye, she wanted to check on me one more time. We talk an instant, and finally, she said these words. "You don't have any idea of how long I have been longing to see you together with Sharleen; it feels like an age. I love you guys forever. I don't know how to halt this feeling." Her words reminded me of my life before now. Carol saw us break apart and find a way back to each other. I did not know that long ago I told her, "Maybe one day, things will change, I hope to learn to be happy in new ways, I hope to find sunshine far from her, but I know I will never forget her." Until now, pain fills my heart to see the many ways life can carry you into unknown paths, how never was a moment away.

Flowers do wither, and leaves do fall. After blue skies, clouds bring rain. People come and go. How can I keep Sharleen forever by my side and make her remember that my love for her will always be the same? Is our nearness all smoke and fog? Just a fantasy in my mind?

I want to repeat every kiss. I want to kiss this girl for the first time every day. Can we do this by falling in love over and over again?

I am there with you, always near you, only for you. This desire to establish me in your thoughts was burning in me. Then a word came to my mind, "Selfless." You may wish to think that you do all for her but if you genuinely want to give love, be selfless.

Life goes by faster than in a blink of an eye. Use the time you have at hand and search for understanding what goes inside your beloved's mind. Take the time and enjoy every instant before all turns into dust.

Sharleen was home before me that night. She was sleeping like a newborn, unsuspecting that I stop to observe the calmness of her face, the peaceful breathing of her body. This girl knew all the demons inside me, and because of her love, my life was worth living. I never felt more passion inside me than when she selflessly gave herself to me.

While we were walking and exchanging kisses, we were making arrangements for Carol's upcoming wedding. It is such happiness when two good people meet and decide to continue living together. Earlier in the day, Sharleen expressed to me her wishes of spending a few more days with Carol to help her with the final arrangements. We agree that she would fly ahead of me, and I would follow her days later.

Did I wish to ask her how long has it been since you and me? For Sharleen, our time together started not months ago, but years ago, so I did not dare to ask. Being with her was like a dream; I wanted this dream to have no end. The days away from me are going to be our first separation since destiny brought us together again.

The day before flying, we met early; it was a rainy day. It was one of those afternoons we enjoyed listening to the city's noise and excitement around us. Later we walked our way home through the park under the rain. She took my hand to warm her face and brush the raindrops off her forehead. I reached for her lips, softly kissing every inch of her face until touching her lips, kissing the only way we knew, fervently. Holding her in my arms, I peacefully contemplate the world around us. The park's lights reflected on the wet tree's leaves, the silence of the empty paths playing with the sound of the rain, and Sharleen's embrace; it was paradise. I know and acknowledge all the simple pleasures life has granted to me.

At home, she kindly whispers words of love as she brushes my hair and caresses me. She knows that I am worried about losing her for some days and was trying to calm my troubled heart. I told her, "I will miss the glow in your eyes looking into mine." There was no need to use words. Hearing Sharleen's voice, my heart becomes calm and tender. I pulled her body closer; our kisses never ceased expressing our hearts.

Early in the morning, we were ready to go to the airport when Sharleen's phone rang. Something was not right. Every time that she looks at me with those eyes, I know what to expect. I understood that Carol was on the other end of the line by the words Sharleen was speaking. After finishing the call, she sat down and explained what Carol told her. Jordan was not the person we thought he was. Jordan has betrayed her and run away, taking some money from her too. Carol felt betrayed by someone she was in love with, and her heart broke.

Everyone undergoes at least one lousy betrayal in life. It is understandable if she was hurt now. Why should she not hate him? He did the worst thing for a person in love. Make her believe that he loved her and then show us all that it is untrue.

Stick a knife in the body, and it heals but injures the heart, and the wound lasts a lifetime. Most of us will try to find a justification, a reason to understand why someone would be so unloving, so life-disrupting, we will do almost anything to avoid having to face these truths. Betrayal is never easy to manage, it is an overwhelming pain, and there is no right way to accept it. I knew Carol; pride will keep her running when love had betrayed her.

Sharleen decided to fly anyway. Somehow she knew that her company was going to help her get better. Real friends help each other. We must never lose hope; the world is not against us. Life has its terrors, but perhaps even the worse terrors are an indication of something good ahead.

It is sad to discover the lies behind a smile and not a single truth behind a promise. Did Jordan get scared from the fact of the relationship turning into something serious, or was he pretending all the time to be something he was not? Could it be he was a narcissist? Some people think that every man that cheats is one. If you say your lover is a narcissist, you are likely describing someone selfish, insensitive, self-centered, and attention-grabbing.

I am confident that Carol did not fail. I am also sure she did not understand why he sabotaged their future. She may never honestly know the reasons for his actions, but the pain will remain from someone who has hidden the genuine intentions.

Chapter XVII

Dark times.

Understand darkness, and you will see the light. Dreaming will be nursed in shades. We need the night to see the stars.

Simple quotes, but each one has validity and truth. Open your mind to everything reality has to offer; never be close-minded if you wish happiness to come your way. A narrow-minded person who cannot look beyond other points of view is in danger of never finding joy in life.

Arriving in Croatia was always sentimentally tied to the past. I saw Sharleen and Carol waiting for me. I needed to hug my beloved girl and tell her I have been in torment until that moment. It was so good to be with her and Carol; after all, the pleasures in life disappear; the memories we bring into existence will prevail forever.

I wanted to tell Sharleen, "I like the break of the morning and noon and nightfall with you." Nothing can replace the lost time, but nothing teaches you more than separation.

Instead of being an admirable beginning looking into Carol's eyes, I saw the sadness of someone that lost trust in a lover. I embraced her and said, "Give love a second chance; you will not be disappointed." She thanked me for coming and added, "Letting go is sometimes the hardest thing."

Maybe it was that brokenness inside Carol that call to mind my fear of losing Sharleen. I know well how loss feels. When people say that love lasts forever, I sadly smile, knowing this not to be true. It is not about the duration; it is about a divine something that puts this love into something way beyond comprehension.

I wished heartily to do or say something to help her. There was nothing I would not do to see her happy again.

She loved him. But he did not know what love was. He was able to pretend, but no words were ever genuine. She gave him her heart; now, she knows he did not have one. He only was with her long enough to take what he needed and went away. Everything she knew about him had been a lie.

It is painful to look at her to see the overwhelming loneliness and isolation of a lover left to fight the betrayal's demons. When you deeply care about someone, you cannot just forget because you learn they failed you.

I knew that the loser was Jordan. He would not have another heart beating for him, but Carol would love again at the right time.

Sharleen likes this city. Opatija is a Croatian coastal city on the Adriatic Sea not far from we used to live. Carol took us to Roko, a nice place she had discovered not long ago. There we were, the three of us on a Saturday, and we loved it! We took place in the lovely ambiance inside because maybe it was a little louder outside, as it was right on the street.

Great fresh food. Homemade pasta, pizzas with a nice fluffy edge.

After long deliberation, I had a pizza Frutti di mare, and Sharleen had risotto with truffles while Carol tried pasta & salad. The homemade bread with garlic, served warm straight out of the oven, was excellent.

I could not control my heart as it pounded out of control in my chest. I was the luckiest man in the world, sitting beside two women that meant my world to me. There is no point in avoiding sad conversations because our thoughts follow us wherever we go and are with us while doing whatever we do. I asked Carol if she was thinking of pressing charges against Jordan; after all, he illegally took values from her she did not give him. She answered me, explaining that right now, she wanted to be crawling alone through shadows if necessary so that one day she would appreciate being on the sunny side of life again. She was not looking for revenge, nor she wished to understand. She just wanted to get over him and be happy once more.

I felt a sense of honor for having such a passionate soul in my life. Carol's light is precious in a world so dark. Sharleen looks at me and then at Carol and said, "Do not let your struggles fill you with fear. After all, it is only in the lightlessness nights that stars shine more brightly."

None of us are just right or wrong, or never wrong and always right. Everybody has good and evil forces working within us. I, however, have stated that for me, good and evil do not exist. It is only our perception of actions by other humans viewing reality with entirely different eyes. We use the expression of good and evil to understand actions too out of our understandings.

I wished I could tell Carol some meaningful words. She was fighting to smile and get over the pain, but I know she was hurt deep inside. One day she would find real love. The love that brings freedom, for there is nothing more liberating than love.

I hold her right hand, and with my left still holding Sharleen's, I said to her, "Soon enough, you will find your soul star, and in that instant, you will not even be looking at the sky."

Turning to Sharleen, I ask her, "I sent you roses yesterday. Did you get them?. " She smiled and said, "I want to be able to love you more than I fear losing you.

Please help me." I could no longer restrain myself and kissed her.

Carol did not let us stay in any other place than at her sea house. Every night, we ate together, having exquisite conversations waiting until dawn and continuing until long into the night. On Sunday, some other people came to the house, and for a moment, sadness seemed to vanish from the world. I was continuously creating occasions to meet new people, to bring new faces into Carol's life. The danger of prolonged hopelessness is its tendency to cloud the ability to see the new beginnings that every day offers.
I counted with Sharleen to organize the most extravagant meetings at work and social reunions after working hours. A wrong group of people would make Carol feel disconnected from the crowd, but the right ones would make her forget about misery and return a smile on her face. Social gatherings can be healing, restoring sources of energy.

So is this it? Is everyone here? I asked Sharleen. "Yea, I guess," she shouted while dancing to the music playing in our ears. Along with the music, the sensation of having fun instantly went through the people we had invited as if it had happened by miracle, and they were all aware that we were throwing a party to avoid any negativity in everyday life. There were no easy days for the two of us, so used to having conventional evening hours, but it was the best thing we could imagine it would help a friend smashed by a deceiving heart. The socializing portion was also not wholly unwelcome, and we had a great time chatting with exciting people yet so utterly aware of each other's presence.

One of many afternoons, we invited George, one of the lawyers involved in the project. It seemed he was the perfect match to divert Carol's attention, at least for the moment. The result was enchanting in every aspect, but a part of me was still apprehensive about the whole thing for countless reasons. We were playing Cupid, and that could bring unexpected results. Only the words I hear George say to Carol brought some peace to my mind. I overheard him say, "We can take our time with everything. Do it right, do it slowly."

Coming to the end of the week, we were ready to fly back, letting destiny take his course. Carol was feeling better and had someone who seemed interested in making her days more becoming.

The night was magnificent. A soft and warm breeze went through the room, bringing memories of the days long gone. Sharleen continues reminiscing about old times, hoping that my memories of our old life will return one day. Sometimes her voice was filled with nostalgia; there is sorrow and pain in everyone's life. Part of her wanted the past to return to me, not accepting living a portion of ourselves unable to return to the present. In the silence, she felt the past, and it was silence because not always we could talk about both remembering details burned in her mind and not available in mine.

Carol would say to us with a lovely smile, "In addition to introducing a new perspective in my life, George gave me several unknown reasons to live in an absurdly superficial way." Above all, I have to thank you guys for being such good friends. I will let you know if anything happens between him and me.

I had to tell Carol, "It is not about whether someone would like to share life with you, but whether the person can recognize how amazing you are."

Adding to my emotional dizziness, Sharleen convinced me that every day spent in Opatija was utterly satisfying.

Turning something horrible into less painful was undoubtedly her doing. There is the irreversible pain of events nobody can erase, but a helping friend brings miracles in the life of someone in need.

The first night days before I arrived, Sharleen told Carol, "I do not care if I need to stay up crying all night long with you. I will stay with you because your pain is known to me." I know of this because Carol was very touched by her honest words and commented on it a few days ago.

I spoke to Donna, a friend of Carol, who last night noted how fantastic George was and went on depicting him as a good-looking and selfless man. Donna was one of the new people that started working after my disappearance. She was energetic and the kind of person you wish to have close during bad times.

Donna was somehow the fighting creature Carol had fortuitously encountered along her path in her active business life. Now both were friends who dealt with also personal matters rather than just attaching importance to job responsibilities. Somehow both began to feel responsible for the mutual welfare.

So much excitement was taking a toll on Sharleen and me. We longed to return to our habitual life. We were ready to go back to our comfortable loving nights, having only us during the night's hours. We missed the quietness of the house, the long walks in the evening, the splendor of having us. During those nights, our lips were for each other, and our eyes were full of dreams. We want our smiles, our kisses, and the touch of our fingers on our bodies. Ours was a world of eternal summer until the winter came.

Perhaps home is not a place but simply a state of mind. It was not necessary to be precisely in that house. The truth is that longing for a place called home lives in all of us.

During our last night before going to sleep, I suggested we take another weekend trip to Greece in a brief moment of whimsy. I wanted her to know all of me and not let anything unknown of my new life. She turned to face me, and our eyes met.

'You are not alone,' said Sharleen and added, "I was never, ever going to let you go alone again anywhere. I am too scare you would disappear."

I whispered, "I wish for a day, just for one more day like the day we spent every hour in bed. Caressing you and kissing you until your beautiful eyes closed to sleep." She said, "The things that fill our lives with comfort and our hearts with joy are those that give meaning to everyday life, and of those, I had plenty."

Almost inaudibly, she said, "I am happy, Tom. I am your girl. I have you. I have everything."

Chapter XVIII


Clouds and rain.


I t was pleasant to be back in our familiar four walls. Today we did not have time for our daily walk to the office. There was too much we left unattended while we were away. It would be a busy day, but we promised each other that the night would be ours. To crave for time and the lack of it is like the sun reflecting everywhere a shadow. We need the sun but not always his shadow. How impossible to have one and not the other.

At the office, everybody was rushing, and the fact that everyone else is doing it does not make it any less insane. We are building a world where everyone becomes abuse somehow. In the pursuit of success, we accept paying the price sometimes too high. I am a convinced soul that motivation is the engine for a better world. It is good to be and stay motivated, but if you are placing so much pressure on yourself that you are making yourself miserable, that is not good.

Does the ocean, the trees, or the mountains make you unhappy? Probably not. It is the ideas of people, always people and systems they created. We are helpless and exposed to copious worries. We are vulnerable, and the pressure of life is most solemn. If we could understand the illusion of separation, all stress would disappear.

Outside, the leaves of the trees cramped and felt. Trees were near the deep yellow of the end of autumn. Coming close to the final days of October is when Sharleen loves to go into nature. She takes inspiration from the watercolor of the leaves on the ground and in the trees.

Some of us died every year when leaves fell from trees, and their branches were bare and turned brown, but an artist looked at the world with different eyes.

To Sharleen, where it was death, she saw a newborn child, where there was snow, saw the sun, and at work kept the same vision. Where there was a problem, she needed a solution.

That afternoon Sharleen was very disappointed by the short sight of many colleagues and artists. Few people are more enthusiastic in life with a colorful and lively attitude than Sharleen. She was never demotivated or hopeless. If she could, she would lift the world alone, and seeing her frustrated was a clear sign of grave concern. One obstacle can infect the whole of the project. It is a rash that runs through our days, our work, our eyesight preoccupied with flaws until we can only see defects. A deficiency works like a virus in the mind of people trying to bring something into the light of reality. The mistake is not knowing enough good to go around and fix the problem. Sharleen and I needed to address the problem and show everyone that there were more than enough creative ideas and solutions at our disposal.

The pressure to be excellent is unrelenting. Believing that this stress will simply disappear once the Website would be operational seems like wishful thinking. Infinite dreams keeping us exhausting hours in the office were part of the package we gladly accepted but now sometimes was too much. My solution is often a long hot shower. When I finish a long shower, it is like my brain has been washed. All the anxiety and negative thoughts are gone with the water. Sharleen was different; she needed to seclude herself in her study and paint.

Nights found us exhausted and regretting not having the liberating time to escape the pressure of work. Sharleen would turn to me and say, "Tell me about those dreadful days when you stood alone on a thin line between dreams and reality. How did you manage not to give up?" I kissed her and ask her, "How did you get through the day when you did not know?" She laughed softly, kissed me back, and pulled me closer to her. Nothing was more comforting than being together to get through the tough times. Words could not explain, and it was pointless to ask.

Everywhere there is a lesson to learn. Behind every stressful situation, we wish for things to be other than they are. Sometimes, we see the solution, find a way out, or realize that the matter is not as important as we thought. It is not stressed circumstances that complicate our life but how we deal with them. Our minds must perceive what is going on, our hearts must hold up under pressure, and finally, we must decide how to react.

If there is no conscious communication, then there is no understanding. Sharleen understood well that to make something possible is more a matter of attitude, the decision, to choose among all the million impossible possibilities, the most satisfying. She came to me and said, "Tom, I know I can bring everybody to agree; we need to get this world together." In a wildly unorthodox way, we resolved to organize a big party to discuss, talk, and get new ideas for the project. Sharleen's art was to understand dealing with people. She knew that solutions do not come from individuals but rather experiences.

I held her hand, and while the worries did not go away, a lucid sense of calm spread over her. We discuss her plans. My opinion was not to have a big party but to invite all the people we knew were not approving our project. We get stronger, not weaker, by entertaining with ideas and people we disagree with. Is the choice to invite and listen to another person even when it is uncomfortable. We can build empathy and gain understanding by engaging sensitively and kindly with controversial ideas and unfamiliar perspectives.

Sharleen accepted my idea, gladly saying, "With you in my life, I feel like I could conquer anything." I know her too well to mention something she would not agree upon. She knew better than me about her colleagues living and working in the art community. Often, even when artists share a passion for art, dealing with others can be uncomfortable. We have ideas that test each other. We have solid and painful disagreements. Rather than being discouraged, we can recognize our discomfort and build from there a better solution.

Before the afternoon was over, we set it all in motion. I would take some time to arrange all the details, but we were confident that it was the best approach to get what we were trying to achieve.

We arrived late at home that night. Abandoning the work reality to live in the memory of our love was the reason we were existing. After getting into more comfortable clothes, I wanted to prepare something to eat. She would keep me company at the kitchen table. We talked about our days, about our future, about whatever came to mind.

In a spontaneous inspiration, Sharleen selected a slow song she loves and asked me to dance with her. We danced like lovers do, and as the song neared the end, she whispered in my ear, "Kiss me like it's the last kiss you will give me." We kissed tenderly at first; the fire of desire developed as a rapid and divine sensation of drunkenness, of madness which gives lovers more happiness in an instant than other men can gather during a whole lifetime.

The moon seems unaware of our return home, but love was on the air that night. We could have tried to push each other away. We could have tried to deny what we felt, but when two hearts have joined and two souls have been reminded of love, there is simply no way fate can keep us apart. Perhaps, the stress of work was forcing us to escape into each other's arms. The intimate short dance, the tender embrace, and the kiss infused the thrill of desire, which we would not have known without days of strain.

That night the moon and the sun shared the sky. I recognize the moment, and I knew, with certainty, I would never feel more right about anything else in my life, that my life was to be beside her. Her eyes were shining and illuminating my heart. She softly said to my ear, "No matter how busy we may be, no matter what dreams we may chase, I will always, always love you." I put my fingers under Sharleen's chin and murmured, "I love you."

Suddenly, there is no longer any difference between achieving a goal or giving up everything we expected. In our eyes, we understood being transitional creatures sharing a world a reality but unattached to the results of our endeavors. We were not haunted by dreams, and our heart was not void because we had reached our hopes and love was in our hearts. We need to escape the fears in our minds. Our souls are the one thing that we cannot escape from.

The nightmare of losing everything was a strange comfort to me. I had confidence that the benefit of such a project would find a way to reality, but neither Sharleen nor I felt devastated if it would not work out.

We need a plan to reach our goals. Knowing we had a good plan gave us satisfaction otherwise, we would lose ourselves in the confusion of the world around us. It would have been nice if problems turned into smoke, but it is nicer when you have to give your best to make things work. Initially, the results are not what we desired or deserved after the effort invested, but it is part of the package we were glad to risk.

Problems are actually blessings in disguise; Any sane person will understand that. Problems had to come, and mistakes were already made. Now, all we had to do is apply the solutions.

Is it not wonderful to travel in time to somewhere in the past? Life continuously kept me aware of changes and circumstances. People get too overwhelmed doing the little things and wonder why they are not getting significant results in the more crucial part of life. My concerns after the accident were demanding all of me. I was facing a substantial dilemma, and it was unavoidable to put all of my efforts into seeking answers. From the actual point of view, my concerns were justified but not necessarily correct. Presumably, in two years, I will look in the same way at my troubles of now, and it will continue to be so at any time in life, and maybe even afterlife included.

The summer is gone. The winter is coming, and after all the happiness Sharleen is giving me, I still find my face with lonely tears. I accepted the departure of Aisling, but I miss our communication. I cry for me, not for her. Dead loved ones are past the crying.

I listened to the beating sound of my heart. I felt the burning blood in my veins and wanted to shout, hoping she could hear me, but only emptiness is where she used to be. This pain and the feeling of the completely powerless me bring me down, and I fade whither like the leaves outside. I love Sharleen, and the hurt of knowing that my feelings of today are going to be hers tomorrow do not let me rest.

I almost burst apart from the longing for a cure so that I do not leave her alone. I would have done anything to ease her suffering, but I knew nothing I might do or say could stop her from being the way she was. Sharleen had touched and nurtured me giving more than I asked for, and I was starting to feel the cold settling, the heat fading, the end coming.

Chapter XIX

Points of view.

I deas are flickering parts of us like candlelight we all carry around, reflecting the personal and unique points of view. All opinions are not equally justified. Some are a great deal more sound, advanced, and well-supported. These opinions should have more value than others, and the wicker or less accepted get blown out by the winds of man.

The idea of inviting people who disagree with our proposal lets them express their thoughts or opinions. That does not grant us the right to deny any sense they might make. The man who never alters his opinion will never become a better version of himself.

This evening would be challenging for us, but we wanted to reinforce our perspective, and probably we will hear what we do not want to hear. Robert and Lucy were two of our project representatives, welcoming our guests. Our team consisted of 18 well-trained specialists ready to explain our view, especially for this night, eager to listen to what people had to say. There are many potential areas of conflict summarized in a few examples.

Lack of communication. If your clients do not understand or misunderstood how we want to offer their products, it will create issues. Always avoid lack of or poor contact; it creates unnecessary problems.

Role confusion. There are many tasks, such as strategizing. If artists are not sure who does what, there can be redundancies or jobs getting overlooked by both sides on the flip side. We have to explain clearly our responsibilities and set the frames for individual freedom of action.

Unclear goals. When everybody works toward a shared goal, it is easier to work together. If it is unclear what the end goal is, or if each one has only its purposes in mind not aligned with each other, it can create conflict and inefficiencies.

Personality and art differences. Each artist tends to attract different types of people. These differences can lead to misunderstanding and tension, almost as if we were speaking other languages. Trying to build a multifaceted institution can be overwhelming but also a rich experience.

The blame game. When something goes wrong, guess who the offender is? Because artists and web developers rarely see eye-to-eye, their understanding and expectations of each other's do not automatically reflect reality. Under a cloud of uncertainty, mishaps tend to get attributed to the other party.

During the evening, I did not see Sharleen but for short encounters. We exchanged some teachings collected so far and continued mingling between our guests. Everyone has their way of expressing themselves. I admit that we all have something to say, but finding ways to say it is where the trouble originates. Some listen, and some never retract their opinions; they love themselves more than they love the truth.

Every one of us judges things based on what is our understanding of the facts. No doubt, widening our knowledge would make us consider differently. People's problem is that everyone believes they can express their opinion, and others must listen to it. Make sure to understand before expressing an opinion.

Although nothing is more peaceful than not having any opinions, our daily doings demand us to stand for some beliefs. I repeat myself saying that there is nothing I can be unchangeably convinced to be correct. I am saying we are unlearning what it denotes to be well informed. Ignorance is not hopeless. The danger is that we could take misguidedness to be knowledge.

A sincere working relationship does not change its colors all the time. We have to stay true to our line and be prepared to adjust for changes. We need more inclusion, partnerships, not partisanship, dedicated just to profit. The future we should aim at is to be better off and change the world. We firmly believed that the best partnerships do not depend on a common goal but on a common path to a more comfortable life.

I could hear interesting opinions like the one from Richard Brannigan, owner of an art gallery, "Alliances are difficult to design precisely because they do not contain a "big boss" but a group of people who do not always hold the same opinion."

The words of a banker were also interesting. The director said, "Choosing a partner is the most important decision most people will make about their business."

So the evening found its way between diverse topics in which people participated harmoniously. And as with any meeting, including the people, we did not skimp on drinks and food. It was never wise to neglect the importance of drinks and small appetizers to keep the atmosphere pleasant.

After the last guest left, there was a sentiment of relief in every one of us. A positive attitude may not solve all of our problems. I could see faces still trying to evaluate the evening, but that is the only option we have to get out of obstacles.

We inspire ourselves to plan every moment and fill our schedules with one activity and obligation after the next. We forget again and again that happiness is often right in front of us. Sharleen came and said, "Please take me home; I am exhausted." I know she was not completely satisfied. Only good people believe they could have done better. I looked at her and told her, "Regardless of how you feel, you deserve to be proud here, and right now, let me take you home."

When your body enters and remains in a state of relaxation, all the world's worries are left behind. No customers to test your limits, no memory to revisit, nothing but calm and Sharleen. My outstretched arms found hers. Even in this exhausted state, my mind finds ways to connect with her. We were indeed home.
It was early in the night when I opened my eyes in the darkness and felt her against my side. Her warm body, the silence, her soft skin, and the sweetness of her sleeping lips converted me into a worshiper of the night.
Early in the morning, I pulled her body closer and brushed her lips with mine. She gradually opened her eyes and smiled softly with a hint of shyness. I looked at her eyes in ways no mirror ever could. She drew a deep, bemused breath and said, "Good morning, sweetheart." I slid my hands up her body and held up her face with my hands. Then, lovingly kissed her.

Today it was my turn to prepare breakfast. I wanted to surprise Sharleen with a very "full English breakfast." Consisted of tea, orange juice, croissants, yogurt, five kinds of cold cereal, fried eggs, eight rashers smoked back bacon, four sausages, two halved tomatoes, baked beans, mushrooms, toast, butter, jam, jelly, and honey. Sharleen started laughing when entering the room. "Are you serious?" she asked. I smiled and said, "Sometimes a girl needed more than coffee and toast in the morning. Today qualified as one of those mornings."

After some time and nutritious breakfast, "You know what?" I asked out of breath, "We are late and about to be in deep trouble. We plausibly better go." Sharleen joked about going back to sleep, but the world was calling for our presence at work.

The first reactions started coming sooner, as expected. There were continuous incoming calls, and to our pleasure, there was a sense of positivity in them.

For what else would we have organized this party besides capturing thoughts that belong to all of us so that we can appreciate our work, understand ourselves, and perhaps, each other.

To stand there, enjoying a good result, brought Lars to my memory. Missing someone is the bounce of an echo of everything beautiful about a person. I hold my breath for a moment, staring at the people rushing from one table to the other. Every one of them submerged in performing their job. To see how life goes by and how little we stop to talk with people we cherish and lost contact with make me decide to call him.

Lars was speechless and glad to hear my voice. Life is so full of unpredictable surprises. He started to talk and explained to me about changes in his life. At some point, he mentioned something that moved me to the verge of tears, maybe even changing me. At the end of the conversation, I could not help promise to take the time and come to visit him in Ireland.

We all like things to be predictable. We expect things to be safe and stay that way for as long as possible. For me, there was no way of knowing how much time I would have before my decline could start.

I wasn't afraid of my illness. I am scared of my past or whatever might bounce out at me.

The whole point of life is never knowing what could happen next.

Sharleen was enthusiastic about the idea of getting to know about my life in Ireland but, considering the circumstances at work, concluded that it would be better if I go alone. I never wanted it to be this way, but she was right. Somebody must take care of business. And with a sad smile, she added, "Even as I hold you close to me, I am letting you go. It is only going to be for two days."

We wanted to spend the night differently. I searched for a new place and make reservations. The restaurant resulted in a delicious little place.

It had a few dishes but all prepared and cooked at the moment. Sharleen had pasta and beans, broccoli flan, and parmesan cream.

We stood, holding each other's faces, memorizing every last detail.

Sharleen looked seriously and said, "This is not a goodbye dinner, okay. There will be no goodbyes, not between us, never again."

After the short call, I had with Lars, my thoughts went again and again back to our conversation. A deep friendship can keep a friend from jumping to negative conclusions, but part of me knew that not everything was going well in Lars's life.

Going back was motivation enough to be excited. I wanted to go back. To say my memories of Ireland were bittersweet happiness was perhaps an understatement. The way all the circumstances had come together was downright magical.

There is a risk that we will lose sight of what our friend is dealing with when we occupy ourselves intensively with our problems. There was too much in which I felt connected to Lars. Without Charlotte or him, my life would have turned to be a somewhat different one.

I don't want him to be one of those people who are quickly forgotten. For me, he was the friend who helped me find a place in the world. So important back then, so unique, so influential, and so valued, but a time later, it cannot just become a vague face and a distant memory. I would not let it be.

Chapter XX


Broken past.


E ven if you wish to forget your past, it remembers
you. After Aisling's death, I promised myself
never to come back to Limerick, but how can you
ever leave a place that meant so much? I guess it is
impossible to leave and impossible to return. This city is
not the same anymore. There are no paths in the park, no
familiar faces, by which I could retrace my steps and bring
the past back. I was trying to convince myself that
memories would not reach my heart.

It was a sweet and bitter taste to be in this city again. I
woke up paralyzed by a waking dread that would not go
away. I could not shake it and dared to name it, afraid it
would confuse my fragile mind.

I knew Lars was waiting for me at his house, but I also
called Shannon and asked her to meet me. She had
agreed and was happy to take time out, so we could talk.
Here in this city, I had unforgettable moments. I wish the
best moments were forever, but trying to remember them,
they always rush by, and now I see how they got out of
hand even though I wanted to hold on to them as long as
possible.

Then I knew that I would dedicate every minute that we
could be together to make Shannon feel happy, to repair
the pain that I had caused her by leaving this part of my
life behind, and now when I returned here, I wanted to
give her what I never knew how to give her. I had left her
mourning alone with nobody at her side to share the pain.

This time Lars was waiting for me. He had a handsome stranger's smile, but Lars was one of the few people in my life who deserved to be called a friend. Something was different in him. A couple of hours ago, he told me that his girlfriend was not with him anymore, but seeing him, I could tell that she broke his heart. I did not want to inquire about the details, but he said, "I never saw it coming; I never thought she would leave." The brief happiness Lars experienced, no matter how short, seemed to be worth the prolonged torture of waking up every day, finding loneliness.

It is sad when the people closest to your heart turn into a bitter memory after both have decided to go separate ways. There was a part of Jennifer in every sentence Lars said. And the price of a memory translated into feelings is the melancholy that it brings.

He was a successful and warm-hearted man searching for a way to forget one big scar of love from a girl that did him wrong.

I was with someone where you did not have to pretend. If you care about somebody, you let that person know you do. I knew Lars was grateful that I had visited him, and I was glad that my presence brought him comfort. Having a friend can be the key to sanity in an insane world spinning out of control.

It is hard to say the right words to someone having the pain of a broken heart. Once one falls in love with true love, a person cannot fall out of love no matter what, and even if someone has hurt us, love will not be easily forgotten. There are wounds that time cannot heal.

Lars said, "Thank you for helping me see how to survive the endless nights." After reflecting for a moment, he added, "I know what happens next is just a compromise with my heart and with my life."

Despite the uncomfortable situation, it was a thrill meeting him and spending a few hours together, indulging in each other's lives. Time does not take away good friends, nor does distance keep us away.

I left that afternoon, his last words still echoing in my head, "Tell Sharleen I love her. We need to get acquainted." I don't know if it is well judged to tell friends that I am going away never to return, but silence is all they hear. People are still waiting, waiting for words to come out.

The road of life turns a little every day, and one day there's an unforeseen bend we did not dream was possible, and you must face a new reality. At times, I wish we could roll back the clock to have a second opportunity and deal differently. We have to forgive ourselves and look for the balance between whom we want to be and who we need to be. I sensed how truly hard it was to see someone you love change right before your eyes. I saw Lars's existence as the best version ever possible. Now he was a shadow of what he was. He was not angry at her for falling in love with another man, nor was he blaming her, but he was in pain because he did not realize the problem until it was too late.

I needed to confront the demands of my soul, asking to revisit places I wanted to burn and toss the ashes into the wind. I went walking in the streets facing unfamiliar eyes, with no names for the faces, and trying not to recognize the voices or what they said. Suddenly I found myself walking a path I could not evade, and my eyes filled with tears. The past was grabbing me, and I was not able to run away. I closed my eyes, and I saw Aisling standing only feet away. I walked closer, close enough to kiss her. Close enough for her to whisper me the most striking words. I heard a voice say, "I loved you when I left you." I opened my eyes, and there was nobody near. I did not know what to do. My head told me to run, to run away, but my feet, stone on the ground, refused to respond.

I closed my eyes again, trying to visualize her. What haunts me most is the clarity with which I could see her and her extraordinary eyes. I could see the pain I put in them. There is no way to mourn love that an accident stole.

Grief reunites you with what you have lost. I remember after Aisling's death, I was following my pain as far as I could go. Walking these streets brought the heartache back. The torment was around to show me that some hurt in my heart would never go away. A cut that never heals.

Avoiding thinking about her was not a solution. There is no such thing as inner peace if you do not face the pain. When I see leaves fall, and in my heart, I know that I am only passing by, some sentiment of peace returns to me, and discomfort disappear.

No matter what you do, right and wrong could happen. Ancient wisdom says that lighting a candle also creates a shadow. You must let what happens to occur. Everything must tend to be equal in your eyes, good and evil, beautiful and ugly, unwise and wise.

I am not a religious person, but I like the Buddhism way of thinking. Buddhism is neither pessimistic nor optimistic. It does not falsely lull you into believing in paradise, nor does it terrorize and agonize you with imaginary fears and sins. It looks at things objectively, "yathābhūtam." I think the appropriate translation would be "as it really is."

Above, the sun was shining vaguely through the cloudy November sky. It was cold and quiet. From a distance, I could see Shannon waiting close to the side of the bridge across the park. We got closer. Then she smiled sweetly as if it was the first time she saw the sun after many decades of winters. I smiled back at her and wondered if she knew what I had seen in her eyes or if she could see the thoughts I was keeping hidden inside me.

I said, "You do not know how good it is to see you. I have never forgotten a woman like you. I must make it clear." Shannon knew how devastated I was after Aisling's death. How hard it was for me to find closure. She embraced me and said, "I am also full of emotions to be here with you. Deep inside, it is nice to remember without a hurt, the heart is hollow."

"Precious Shannon," I whispered. "You made a promise between your heart, your soul, and Aisling, and you both sealed it with love" How can I think you wouldn't understand my pain? She blinked, looking moved by my words. A tear froze on her cheek from where I gently wiped it with my fingers.

Her beautiful eyes widened and then narrowed, "You will not always see me so emotional," she said sweetly.

We want to stroll to remember old times, but it was cold, so we went to a coffee house and ordered something hot to drink.

I told him that when I left, I was falling apart, one part after another. Falling to the ground like snow, half of me was already on the pavement, waiting for the other half to follow. My memories had voices too. Often sad ones who longed for me like arms in the dark. Nothing was able to take my pain away. I was in a dark place, but I was constantly reminded of her when I thought of light.

I told how I met Carol and how my memories slowly returned to me. I said to her, "Finding my memories of a forgotten world never made me forget you or Aisling. Finding love again in the sea of my emotions was like holding a pearl. Very difficult to find, but very valuable and still beautiful."

Noticing that the conversation was only on me, I asked Shannon to tell me about her.

She told me that her mind repressed specific traumas for sheer survival reasons. She said in a calm voice: "I don't know why, but whenever it rains, I remember her, not as a tear that falls, but as someone who loved the rain and enjoyed every drop."

Shannon's last words about Aisling that afternoon were, "Often, in the still of the night, Aisling comes back to me. So many fond memories bring the light of her in the darkness surrounding me, reminiscing older days when she was around me with her smiles, tears of happiness, boyfriend drama." That words were said by her with a smile on her face and with love on her tongue. She told me how she missed her bright eyes of hers now dimmed and gone.

Shannon's joyous hearts clearly broke, and she missed her.

It was cold outside, but we wanted to repeat our traditional stroll the way we used to do. I brought her home, kissed her goodbye, and left with a bitter taste and a tight throat. Some goodbyes leave a void that time will never fill again.

It was a long day, now at the airport waiting for my flight, I had some time to relax. I went walking around the dutty-free shops looking for something to bring to Sharleen. I believe the most precious gift you could ever give your woman is your time, attention, your love, and occasionally the pair of porcelain earrings I was buying.

Once, I embraced the pain of losing Aisling. It was like staring at the sun until my eyes were blinded. I was not able to see that I had forgotten the moon and the stars. I may never change, but being forever stuck in the past was not what she wished.

I know she honestly wanted me to be happy to be loved. Next time I see Aisling, I hope she will tell me, "I loved you when I left you, but I never forgot you." I would again look at her eyes, and I will not see pain but love.

Chapter XXI

Equal value.

Arriving at Bologna's airport, I wanted to call Sharleen, but I decided to surprise her. She knew I was coming but not the exact time. When I entered the house, I found her crying on a sofa in the living room. She brushed her tears and came running my way to hug me tenderly. At a certain point, Sharleen puts her arms around me and starts murmuring things into my ear, "I know you never left my heart, but now I welcome the part that left." I kissed her sweet lips. It was clear to me that her lips have tasted tears caused by me. Maybe the salt of tears produces the best kissing lips. I asked if everything was OK. She just said, "No, nothing is." I held her with my arm, and my other hand touched her cheek, wiping her tears with my thumb. She pointed to a letter she left on the table. The latest result came with negative news. Words. Just tiny black marks on paper. Words that can change your way, your life. Bad news that affects everybody and alters relationships.

"I consciously lied when I told you that I would accept. I am not ready to see you go away," Sharleen then said with sad eyes. I did not know what to do. I did not want to cry. I tried to be tough to hold tears back, but that only made it difficult to breathe. I wanted Sharleen to feel better, not to let her see me cry. I just wanted to hold the tears, but they disobey me. To deny being emotional in that instant was to deny the beating in my heart. Our tears begin where our words stop expressing the pain we feel.

I said, "Sometimes it is better to feel. You have to cry before you can smile again." Sadness was coming over me, and slow tears ran from my eyes.

I part my lips, but no words were able to come out. Essentially, I wanted to hold Sharleen in my arms until I knew she would be OK. Finally, some words came out, and I said, "Cry as much as you want to, but let promise us that when we finished, we never cry for the same reason again." The tears were streaming down her face, but I made no effort to brush them away.

Crying doesn't mean you're weak; it is what you need to do to get healthy again.

I will always see the love in Sharleen's eyes. She whispered, "Crying is always easier in the dark, and when the tears blur, your vision is when you see clearly. Separation shall not silhouette beats getting helpless in my heart." And added, "I will never witness the ocean without thinking of you."

In bed, I throw my arm around her neck and press her cheek against mine. She silently cried until the weight of the day and the overwhelming feeling of sleepiness overcame her. Looking at Sharleen tenderly sleep, a tear escaped my eye, darkening her blue nightwear.

From now on, little by little, I must prepare myself to face death. Living and dying are part of life, in a sense, of equal value.

There is hardly any way to prepare for how pretty a place is before you must leave, especially when a return is out of sight.

Suspicion washed over me when I first got my headaches again, but I did not want to worry Sharleen. I did not want to leave her, but this was it.

I wonder why I thought that the only one who was alone is the person who is parting, being that the people who are left behind would undoubtedly feel the same or even worst. I would close my eyes and fade into nothingness. Waking up not remembering was torture. Never waking up is a blessing.

FSC
www.fsc.org
MIX
Papier | Fördert
gute Waldnutzung
FSC® C083411

Zeitfracht Medien GmbH
Ferdinand-Jühlke-Straße 7
99095 Erfurt, Deutschland
produktsicherheit@kolibri360.de